STRANGER'S FLOWERS

KEMAL TABYLDY

Stranger's Flowers
Copyright © 2024 by Kemal Tabyldy.

MILTON & HUGO L.L.C.
4407 Park Ave., Suite 5
Union City, NJ 07087, USA

Website: *www. miltonandhugo.com*
Hotline: *1- 888-778-0033*
Email: *info@miltonandhugo.com*

Ordering Information:
Quantity sales. Special discounts are granted to corporations, associations, and other organizations. For more information on these discounts, please reach out to the publisher using the contact information provided above.

Library of Congress Control Number: 2024918941
ISBN-13:   979-8-89285-209-8   [Paperback Edition]
                979-8-89285-210-4   [Hardback Edition]
                979-8-89285-211-1   [Digital Edition]

Rev. date: 08/23/2024

"A person whose purpose in life is rooted in loving others has never truly known love for himself…"

CONTENTS

Floral Wallpaper

Chapter 1... 3
Chapter 2... 6
Chapter 3...14
Chapter 4...38
Chapter 5...57

Withered Rose

Chapter 1...87
Chapter 2..129
Chapter 3..171

Epilogue 221
About the Author 237

FLORAL WALLPAPER

Kemal Tabyldy and Alisha Aktayeva

CHAPTER

1

"Have you ever wondered what your life might have been like if you hadn't succumbed to the demons of your past?" the doctor asked, his voice smooth and oddly compelling, his eyes boring into Grace's.

Grace barely glanced away from the vase filled with unnervingly perfect flowers, their beauty almost too vivid, too alive.

"Would your life be a little different, or drastically changed?" the doctor repeated, a hint of a smile playing on his lips, almost as if he already knew the answer.

"Yes, maybe," she replied uncertainly.

The room, decorated in a Provencal style, appeared warm and inviting, yet to Grace, it seemed off, as if the cozy facade was hiding something darker. Despite the bright and cheerful interior, an oppressive atmosphere lingered, making the air feel heavy.

"How old are you?" the doctor asked, his patience thinning.

"Seventeen," Grace replied. "But tomorrow, I'll be eighteen and finally able to quit your stupid therapies," she muttered, her voice tinged with defiance.

"Hmm..." The doctor paused, jotting something in his notes with a sleek, black pen that seemed too elegant for such mundane tasks. "Would you like to discuss how your life might change?" he asked again.

Grace considered leaving the office. The repetitive questions were draining her, sapping her desire to share. Taking a deep breath, she decided to stay.

"Doctor, I don't want to answer your questions, attend your useless sessions, or talk to my annoying guardians about them. So can we just sit in silence? You can think about how to help those you actually can. I'll put on headphones, and you won't even notice me." Grace reached for her white headphones, mentally selecting a song.

"Miss Freeman..." the doctor said, his tone suddenly icy, sending a chill down Grace's spine.

"Don't call me that!" Grace snapped, her irritation flaring.

A heavy silence filled the room. The doctor studied her carefully, his gaze penetrating, almost as if he could see straight into her soul. A stubborn girl would need a special approach.

"Grace..." He paused, as if savoring the moment. "I need to make a report on our conversations. Your resistance only prolongs our sessions, which your guardians have insisted upon. Until we establish a relationship, even at eighteen, you won't be able to stop seeing me. Your guardians have signed a contract for 'full agreement.' Once you turn eighteen, the state will inquire about our sessions. Cooperate. It's in your best interest."

Grace diverted her eyes to the delicate, light wallpaper. The flowers, swirling in a peaceful dance, offered her a semblance of calm. When she felt overwhelmed, she focused on them, finding solace in their intricate designs. The expertly painted flowers on the burgundy walls had a soothing effect. Maybe the doctor was right; maybe it was worth trying to move forward. It seemed logical, even if her heart wasn't in it.

"Okay," she said reluctantly. "Yes, I think my life would be better if I didn't live with the Freemans. My life would be better if I were the star of the school, surrounded by attention and popularity. My life would be better if I had someone I could trust who loved and cared for me." She clenched her fists mentally, her words spilling out.

The doctor noted something down. "It's good that you acknowledge what you're missing and feel dissatisfied with in your life. But my question was different, wasn't it? I asked if your life could have been better if you hadn't clung to the past. Your biological parents, for example. Why do you react so aggressively when it comes to the Freemans, your guardians?"

Grace reluctantly listened, her gaze returning to the vase of flowers. As a child, her mother would sit with her on a soft sofa, opening a small, elegant book with a daisy on the cover, discussing the meanings and properties of flowers. Warm memories echoed in her chest; perhaps that's why the wallpaper and vase helped her block out negative emotions.

She noticed a bright coral shade with black specks scattered on the petals. "Tiger Lily" came to mind. Grace looked back at the doctor, a question forming.

"You know, in all this time, I still haven't asked your name..." she remarked.

The doctor smiled.

"Samuel, but you can call me Sam."

For a moment, doubt flickered in her eyes. She was obviously contemplating something important. Finally, Grace stared at the doctor, scrutinizing his face. Exhaling, she said trustingly, "Okay, Sam, let's cooperate."

CHAPTER

2

The doctor's warm smile, combined with his dispassionate gaze, made Grace uneasy. Even though she was reluctant to share anything personal, she knew that revealing her true feelings might be the only way to end these frustrating therapy sessions.

"So, what's stopping you from enjoying your life?" Sam asked smoothly, his voice calm yet compelling. As he prepared to take notes in his notebook, his icy blue eyes seemed to pierce through Grace. After a moment of tense silence, Grace sighed and tried to focus on her inner feelings. The sight of the lilies in the room—bright and almost unnervingly perfect—helped her drift back to her childhood.

"My life used to be like a fairy tale… Dad would come home from work every day with a bar of my favorite milk chocolate. Even though Mom was against it, saying it was too sugary, he'd just smile and give it to me." Grace smiled sadly as she remembered those simpler times, when her biggest worries were a bad grade in math and her parents' refusal to let her keep a pet.

Sam scribbled in his notebook with a steady, almost mechanical precision. He listened intently, his gaze unwavering and strangely intense.

—⁓—

The dressing table in Grace's room was a jumble of cosmetics and accessories. She added the final touches to her makeup, carefully applying black mascara while her mouth remained slightly open in concentration. The brown eyeshadow highlighted her warm, honey-toned eyes, making them more vivid. Her golden curls fell gracefully over her shoulders, and the blue dress she wore completed her delicate look.

As Grace was finishing up, her mom appeared in the doorway, leaning casually against the frame. She took in Grace's appearance with a smile, admiring her daughter's resemblance to her father. Though Grace's features were softer, they clearly reflected her dad's.

"What time is it?" Grace asked, glancing anxiously at the clock.

"Fifteen minutes to six," her mom replied.

"Shoot! I'm running late! Can you help me?" Grace asked, her eyes wide with urgency.

"Of course," her mom said with a chuckle, amused by Grace's frantic tone.

Lillian motioned for Grace to turn around while she zipped up her daughter's dress.

"What gift did you prepare for Sarah?" she asked.

"I put together a photo diary from the last three years," Grace said cheerfully.

"Can I see it?" her mom asked with interest.

"Sure!" Grace responded, retrieving a small leather-bound book from a gift box.

Her mom's face lit up as she flipped through the pages, her eyes softening at the photos of Grace and her best friend, filled with joyful memories. Lillian looked up with a sudden realization. "Oh, I forgot to put on my makeup. I'll be quick."

Grace gave her reflection one last approving glance and headed towards her room to write a birthday message for Sarah.

A series of sharp, erratic knocks at the window startled her. Her heart raced as the sound echoed through the quiet house. It was rhythmic and insistent. She hesitated, her pulse quickening, then cautiously approached the window, peering outside. The darkness beyond offered no answers.

Her fear intensified. She glanced back, her breath catching in her throat. The knocking grew louder, more urgent. Grace approached the window slowly, her hands trembling.

"Dad?!" she called out, her voice shaky.

She nearly jumped out of her skin when her father appeared behind her. "I called you three times. What's wrong? Why were you shouting?"

"Someone was throwing rocks at my window!" Grace said, her voice barely above a whisper.

Her dad stepped outside to check, his expression growing more concerned. "Hmm, there's no one here. Maybe it was just someone passing by?"

Grace forced a nervous laugh. "Yeah, maybe."

"Come on, put your shoes on. We need to get going," her dad said, guiding her downstairs.

Excitement surged through Grace as she hurried down the stairs.

"Mam, Dad, are you ready?" she called from the second floor.

"Yes, honey, your dad's almost ready. You can sit down while I iron his jacket. We'll be out in five minutes," Lillian shouted back.

Grace rolled her eyes playfully and went outside to the car. As she opened the back door, she froze. A stranger stood alarmingly close to her window, hurling stones with disturbing persistence. He had a disheveled appearance with torn clothes, tangled hair, and an overall unkempt demeanor that made her skin crawl.

The stranger noticed her and stopped, his eyes locking with hers. He slowly extended a hand, pointing at the house. "My lady, I hope you'll pardon the intrusion. Do you live here?"

"Yes," Grace replied, her voice trembling with unease.

"And the car you're near—does it belong to the owners of this house? Lillian and Frank Bailey?" the stranger asked, his voice carrying an unsettling tone.

Grace's discomfort grew. "How do you know about my parents? And why were you throwing rocks?"

"Yes, that's right," the stranger said, his smile widening into something eerie. "I threw a few stones to get their attention. It's important that I speak with them. Could you please call them for me?"

Grace's fingers gripped the car door handle tightly, her knuckles white. "Why?"

"If you look at the right rear wheel of the car," he said, his smile stretching unnervingly, "you'll notice it's slightly deflated. This poses a significant risk to everyone on the road."

The stranger's words lingered ominously. Grace stared at him, her mind racing. "What does this guy know about cars? And why is he here?"

As Grace heard the front door open, she turned to call out, "Mom! Dad! He's the one who threw rocks at my window!"

Her parents looked around, puzzled. "Honey, there's no one here."

When Grace looked back, the stranger had vanished. Panic surged through her. "What...? He was right here! Never mind, let's go to Sarah's. We're running late."

Mr. Bailey started the engine, and the family set off.

The drive resonated with the hum of the engine and the soft strains of the radio. Suddenly, a deafening bang erupted from the front of the car, rocking the vehicle. The car lurched and swerved, engulfing Grace's world in chaos.

The impact was bone-jarring. Grace's head slammed against the seat, and the car spun wildly before it skidded to a halt. The sound of crumpling metal and shattering glass echoed in her ears.

"Grace!" Lillian's voice pierced through the haze.

Grace struggled to open her eyes, but the pain was overwhelming. Red and blue lights flashed through the cracks of the shattered window. The acrid smell of smoke filled the air. Grace's head throbbed painfully, and she felt something warm and sticky flowing down her face. She touched it and saw her fingers smeared with blood.

"Get the crowbar! The door won't open! We need to break the glass!" someone shouted, their voice distorted by the ringing in Grace's ears.

Reality blurred as Grace's consciousness wavered, slipping into a dark void once again.

—⚊—

A barely noticeable tear flowed down her pale cheek. The terrible images in her memory alternated one after another and caused a sharp pain in the girl's heart.

"No one could have imagined that such a thing could happen... so suddenly, and change my life beyond recognition..." A lump in her throat tightened, making her words nearly inaudible. "On the last day, we laughed and cooked breakfast to the Beatles songs. The scrambled eggs burned, and Mom started scolding Dad for being inattentive. He suddenly laughed, and I picked up his laugh. Mom couldn't stay gloomy for long. Oh, how she smiled at him afterwards..." The tenderness in Grace's eyes and the trembling lips created a strange contrast.

"At the hospital, I was told our car had overturned on the turn home. The tire burst, and we crashed into a tree at high speed. My parents were already dead in the car," she choked on the words, another tear slipping down her face.

"But over time, you get used to everything."

Her brown eyes turned cold again, losing their former spark. Grace, familiar to the doctor, had returned.

- "That stranger was talking about this wheel... if only I..." Grace raised her tear-filled eyes and exhaled deeply, struggling to regain control of her emotions. With a determined effort, she met Sam's gaze and said,

- "And what can you do about it, Doctor?!" Her lips twisted into a bitter, ironic smile.

Ignoring the sarcastic tone, Sam wrote something in his notebook and replied,

"Maybe you should have told your parents about this stranger..."

Grace burst into a loud, derisive laugh, cutting him off.

- "Maybe you shouldn't have... Maybe you should have," Sam continued, his tone steady. "How could you have known? No one could have predicted such a turn of events..." After a brief pause, he added, "... of events."

"Yes, but I did nothing. I ignored the stranger. I didn't tell my parents. I forgot the diary for Sarah. I'm the only one left. I live with the Freemans. I can't have breakfast with my actual parents. I can't do anything!" Grace's frustration poured out.

"Grace, everything will be alright," Sam said coldly. "We're here to help you. Continue your story. How was your relationship with Sarah? How did you cope with losing your parents?" he asked, jotting notes in his notebook.

The questions came rapidly, leaving Grace increasingly disoriented. She took a deep breath, her gaze falling on the marigolds in the vase. The bright flowers seemed almost mocking in their cheerfulness, contrasting sharply with her inner turmoil. The room felt too small, the air too heavy.

Grace's chest tightened, the weight of her grief and frustration becoming almost unbearable. The sterile environment of the office felt stifling, and she could barely breathe. Her eyes flitted to the marigolds, and a fleeting thought crossed her mind—if only she had acted differently.

"I'm sorry," she said, her voice breaking. "I need a break."

As she stood up, the room seemed to close in on her, amplifying her distress. She moved toward the door with heavy steps, her mind a tumult of confusion and frustration. The bathroom offered a momentary refuge from the cold, clinical space of the office. She needed to confront her reflection, to regain a sense of calm before returning to the uncomfortable scrutiny of her emotions.

Inside the bathroom, Grace cupped cold water in her hands and splashed her face, trying to refresh herself. Leaning on the sink, she stared blankly at her reflection. Her once warm eyes were now dimmed by exhaustion and sorrow. Dark circles underlined her eyes, evidence of sleepless nights and endless thoughts. Her gaze, once full of life, was now marked by a growing hatred of the image in front of her. Tears welled up and fell into the sink as the bathroom door opened suddenly.

"Dr. Sam?" a woman who was touching up her makeup asked with a forced cheerfulness.

"Yes," Grace replied with a tired smile.

"Don't worry, it's all going to be okay. I was his first client when I had issues with my husband," the woman said with a knowing smile. "Now, I can say with confidence that the therapy worked wonders. I've realized my worth. I'm successful, beautiful, smart, and stronger than ever. Life has become so much easier," she continued.

Grace wiped away her tears and looked at the woman more closely. There was something both enigmatic and slightly unnerving about her demeanor.

"Trust me, dear, he's really good. Extremely... good..."

"I hope you're right," Grace said, raising an eyebrow.

"Lilith," the woman said, extending her hand in greeting.

Grace shook Lilith's hand with a tentative smile.

"Alright then, good luck!" Lilith gave one last satisfied glance in the mirror, straightened her hair, and left, closing the door behind her.

Grace remained by the sink, replaying the brief encounter in her mind. She patted her cheeks gently and then walked back to the study with the flowered wallpaper, trying to compose herself.

CHAPTER

3

The Doctor, still sitting in his maroon leather armchair, made notes in his notebook while crossing his legs.

Grace paused at the doorway, her gaze drifting around the office. While pausing at the doorway, Grace's gaze drifted around the office and she noticed something peculiar: the tiny crevices in the frame were not filled with dust but soot. "A recent fire?" she wondered silently, or perhaps he smokes, she mused, glancing at the doctor. Her eyes moved downward, and she observed the floor outside was wood, but inside, it was polished red marble, so shiny it reflected her image in crimson tones. "The door frame is dirty, but the floor is meticulously clean. Quite the contrast," she noted to herself.

The room had a curious mix of elements. It felt warm inside, but the armchair she sat in was oddly cold. The wool carpet between their chairs beckoned for comfort, yet it felt stale and prickly. The Doctor's smile, though warm, couldn't mask the coldness lurking behind his eyes. Samuel wanted to help Grace, while Grace wanted to escape Samuel.

As Grace stepped into the room, she felt a subtle shift from the cooler world outside to the slightly warmer interior. It was as if the room itself was trying to lure her into a false sense of security while hiding something beneath its surface.

"Miss Bailey!" the Doctor called out as soon as Grace crossed the threshold. "Please, have a seat," he said with a smile, gesturing to the armchair.

Grace settled into the chair with a faint smile, thinking, "Well, at least he's not Freeman. Am I really that loud entering room?"

"How are you? I hope..." Sam began.

"Let's cut to the chase, Sam," Grace interrupted abruptly.

"As you wish," Sam replied, his tone remaining even.

"How did your parents' death affect your relationship with Sarah? And how did you cope with the loss?"

The Doctor readied his notebook, his expression attentive.

"After I woke up and received the news of my parents' deaths..." Grace paused, her throat tightening. Her heart ached with the weight of unshed tears. "Strangely enough, I didn't feel anything. It was like I was numb. Two days passed in a blur. I ate the food the nurses brought me in silence, stared at the ceiling. Nothing gave me joy or sadness. I didn't even need to feel," she blurted, her voice flat. "On the third day, Sarah burst into the room with her parents and threw herself at me, hugging me tightly."

Grace's voice wavered, and she swallowed hard, trying to push down the rising tide of guilt and sorrow. "I felt so disconnected from everything, like I was just floating in a void. Sarah's hug was the first thing that made me feel anything, but even that... it just felt like a distant echo."

Sam's eyes gleamed with a cold, almost predatory interest. "And how did that make you feel, reconnecting with Sarah?"

Grace's brow furrowed, the memory painful. "It made me feel... guilty. Like I didn't deserve to feel anything good after what happened. I kept thinking about that stranger... how he warned us about the wheel. If only I had said something..."

Sam's smile remained, but there was an unsettling intensity in his gaze. "Perhaps you should have. Or perhaps it was fate. You couldn't have known what would happen."

Grace's heart pounded as she looked into Sam's eyes, feeling a chill that seemed to pierce her very soul. She shook her head, trying to clear the thoughts. "I can't help but think that maybe if I'd done something differently, they'd still be here. And now I have to live with that."

Sam's voice exuded an eerie sense of serenity. "Guilt can be a powerful force, Grace. But it can also be a path to redemption."

Grace's eyes widened slightly at his words. "Redemption?" she echoed, feeling a shiver run down her spine.

"Yes," Sam said softly, leaning forward. "We all seek redemption for our actions, whether we realize it or not. Sometimes, we pave the path to redemption with our darkest fears and deepest regrets.

Grace felt a knot in her stomach, the room's warmth now suffocating. "I didn't want to feel anything, but now it's like everything is crashing down on me," she confessed, her voice barely a whisper.

Sam's gaze seemed to bore into her. "Grace, you must confront these feelings to move forward. Only by facing them can you find peace."

Grace's eyes were unfocused, staring into the distance as she recounted the memory. The room's suffocating warmth seemed to close in on her, intensifying her feelings of guilt and despondency.

"I didn't cry," Grace said softly, her voice barely above a whisper. "I couldn't cry. It was like I was... empty. Nothing mattered. Just... nothing."

Sam leaned forward slightly, his eyes narrowing as he listened. "It's not uncommon to feel numb after such a traumatic event. It's your mind's way of protecting you from the overwhelming pain."

Grace's gaze flickered to the polished red marble floor, her reflection distorted and fragmented. "Sarah and her parents tried to help. They said they'd take care of me, but it didn't change how I felt. I just... wanted to be left alone."

Sam's voice was gentle, yet there was an undercurrent of something deeper, almost sinister. "Isolation can be both a refuge and a prison. You felt safe in your solitude, but it also trapped you in your grief."

Grace shivered despite the warmth of the room. "I felt like I didn't deserve to feel anything good. That maybe... if I'd done something different, they'd still be here."

Sam's smile was faint, almost imperceptible. "Guilt is a heavy burden to bear, Grace. But it's also a path. A path to understanding and, perhaps, redemption."

Grace's heart ached, and she took a deep breath, trying to steady herself. "I hope you're right," she murmured.

"Trust me," Sam said, his voice low and soothing. "Facing your demons is the first step to finding peace."

Grace really didn't feel any emotion. The constant devastated look and a certain absent stare spoke of the child's severe trauma. Thoughts did not bother her, or rather, she did not even think about the loss. She did not think about where she would live, how she would live, with what money... absolute emptiness.

For the first time, the little girl felt the aching longing of loneliness. Conversations with nurses, doctors, and the police inspector did not bring any comfort. There was no hint of it.

"How are you?" Sarah asked anxiously, squeezing her friend's shoulders tightly.

"Grace, don't worry. Monica and I have decided that we can take custody of you," Sarah's father, William, said with a warm, soothing smile.

"Yes, that's why everything will be fine. After the doctors let you go, we'll come. We'll pick up all the things from your home on the way," his wife Monica continued for William.

"Thank you," Grace said hollowly to her "new" parents, who were already standing by the door.

"How are you?" Sarah asked again, carefully tucking a stray curl of her friend's hair behind her ear.

Grace, despite her best efforts, couldn't get anything out in response. She didn't need anyone. And how could she feel? It would probably be right to throw a tantrum, burst into tears, and cry and cry until she had no strength left. Oh, yes, there is none. Therefore, why doesn't everyone just leave her alone?

"Well," William said, clearing his throat. "Get well, we'll see you soon." Placing her hand on Grace's shoulder, Monica hinted with a glance at Sarah to leave the room.

Grace found herself alone again, her eyes fixated on the receding silhouettes of her new guardians as they led Sarah away. The small window framed their departure, creating an almost surreal picture that seemed distant and disconnected from her reality. The sight of their retreating figures, hand in hand, only deepened her sense of isolation.

As the door clicked shut, the room seemed to grow colder, the sterile walls closing in around her. Grace's vision blurred slightly as she stared at the moving figures through the window, her mind numb and heavy. She watched them until they were completely out of sight, the empty hallway beyond reflecting the emptiness she felt inside.

A profound sense of coldness wrapped around her heart, squeezing it tightly. It was as if the warmth of human connection was being systematically stripped away, leaving behind only a void. The longing for her parents, the ache of their absence, settled deep in her chest, a constant, gnawing pain that refused to abate.

Feelings of inferiority seeped into her thoughts. She questioned her worth and her place in the world after everything familiar had been ripped away. What right did she have to feel joy or comfort when her parents were gone? The loneliness was suffocating, a silent scream trapped within her.

Unable to hold back any longer, a single, lonely tear escaped the corner of her eye, tracing a slow path down her cheek. It was a tear of profound sorrow, of helplessness, and of a grief too vast for words. The tear fell silent, splashing onto the stark white sheets of the hospital bed, a small but poignant testament to her overwhelming despondency.

Grace remained there, enveloped in her solitary grief, feeling more alone than she ever had before.

—⚬—

It was a scorching July day, the sun blinding and relentless, driving everyone to seek refuge in the cool shade. In the middle of the day, right on schedule, a pink ice-cream van drove past the houses, its light, alluring melody filling the air and heralding sweet, cool relief. The children eagerly expected this daily treat, but on this particular day...

"Mam, she took my shovel!" a girl, covered in sand, ran up to her mother in hysterics. Her hair stuck out in absurd directions, and her tear-streaked face reflected the deepest resentment and anger.

"You destroyed my castle first!" an equally disheveled child shouted after her, their little faces red with indignation. Both girls stood there, arms crossed over their chests, glaring at each other.

Little Grace had accidentally stepped on the sandcastle of the neighbor's girl, Sarah, who, in a fit of rage, had snatched away Grace's shovel. What began as a fierce confrontation soon turned into a teary standoff.

After a long, tearful showdown, the girls ran hand in hand toward the ice-cream van, which was about to leave for its next location.

"Which ice cream do you like the most?" Grace asked her new friend, her eyes glowing with excitement. Just moments ago, she had considered Sarah her sworn enemy, but now...

Fortunately, there was no better way to reconcile than a pinky promise. With one little shake, they let go of all resentments.

"Caramel," Sarah replied, her golden hair glowing in the sun. "And you?"

"Chocolate, of course! It's the best!" Grace exclaimed with enthusiasm. "Do you want to come to my house afterward? We can play with dolls and build a fort out of chairs and blankets."

Sarah's face lit up with a broad smile. "Come on!" she nodded eagerly.

And so, the two girls, who had just met and fought over a sandcastle, found themselves bound by the unbreakable bond of shared ice cream, laughter, and the promise of endless playdates.

—◦◦◦—

"We have been friends since childhood. We went to the same school, were fond of music, and adored Agatha Christie's detectives and pastries. I thought nothing could ruin our friendship. But, as it turns out, you shouldn't underestimate yourself." Grace's face remained impassive, masking the storm of emotions beneath.

"Miss Bailey, can you hear me?" Dr. Sam's voice cut through her reverie.

"Oh, yes, I was thinking. What did you say?" Grace asked, snapping back to the present.

"You withdraw into yourself," the doctor observed, his tone both interested and slightly mocking. "Would you like to practice some breathing exercises to help you focus?"

Grace exhaled sharply, mimicking the "practicing breathing" that Sam often teased her about. "I'm sorry, I'll continue," she replied with a hint of irritation.

Settling back, Sam prepared to write, a smile playing on his lips.

"For the first time after their death, I was in a state of shock and couldn't accept what had happened. I couldn't believe they were just... gone. Later, realization hit, and it brought endless tears, breakdowns, and tantrums. But, I coped, accepted reality, and continued to live without them. Sarah was always with me. Her parents took custody of me, and they treated me well because their daughter and I had grown up together. The issue of adoption was quickly resolved. That was the main mistake..."

Grace's gaze drifted to a bouquet of marigolds on the table. Their vibrant, sun-like blooms seemed both out of place and eerily fitting in the room's oppressive atmosphere. The flowers' familiar presence stirred something within her, prompting her to delve deeper into her memories of Sarah.

"Sarah was my rock," Grace continued. "She never left my side, not once. Her parents, William and Monica, were like second parents to me. They took me in without hesitation, and for a while, it seemed like everything might be okay. But living with them, being in Sarah's home, it was a constant reminder of what I had lost. It was like I was living in a shadow, always trying to fit in, but never quite managing."

Grace's voice trembled slightly, the weight of her emotions pressing down on her. "We did everything together, just like before. But there was this... unspoken thing between us. This knowledge that things would never be the same. We both tried to ignore it, to pretend that everything was fine. But it wasn't. I could never fully escape the guilt, the feeling that I was intruding on their family, that I didn't really belong."

Dr. Sam's pen scratched against the paper, capturing every word. "How did Sarah handle this? Did she ever talk to you about it?"

Grace shook her head. "No, we never talked about it. We just kept going, day after day. Sarah was always so supportive, always trying to cheer me up. But I could see the strain on her too. She was carrying my pain and her own."

Her eyes welled up with tears, but she blinked them away. "I didn't want to burden her, but I couldn't help it. I needed her, and she was there for me. But it wasn't fair to her. It wasn't fair to any of us."

Grace fell silent, the memories swirling around her like a dark cloud. The marigolds seemed to mock her, their bright faces a stark contrast to the darkness she felt inside.

—w—

"Girls, wake up, you're going to be late for school," Sarah's mom, Monica, shouted from the kitchen. The smell of fried eggs and sausages wafted through the house.

Grace immediately got out of bed and ran to wake Sarah, who was still fast asleep. Sarah could sleep through anything, Grace thought with a smile as she shook her friend gently.

Sarah opened her eyes with difficulty and looked at Grace, a gentle smile spreading across her face. "Good morning, Donut!"

"Donut" was Sarah's affectionate nickname for Grace because of her love for round, iced donuts. In turn, Grace had nicknamed Sarah "Caramel" because of her friend's bright brown eyes and love for caramel ice cream.

"Don't call me that," Grace laughed, giving Sarah a playful shove.

It was the first day of school. The golden hues of autumn had replaced the warm summer days. The air was cooler, the sky a piercing blue, and the leaves had turned to vibrant shades of yellow, red, and gold.

The girls sat down at their desks as the bell rang. The teacher introduced the new students, and the lesson began.

"Let's start," the teacher said enthusiastically, drawing circles on the blackboard. "As you remember, the nucleus of an atom consists of..."

A latecomer entered the room, interrupting the teacher. Grace immediately noticed that the boy didn't have a backpack or notebook, just a pen he was twirling.

"Hello!" he greeted with a sarcastic smile.

"Two minutes late, Andrew," the teacher said, displeased.

"Yes, yes, I know," Andrew replied comically as he walked to his desk. "Oh, by the way," he pointed to the blackboard, "Protons and neutrons."

"Sit down and don't distract the class," the teacher said angrily.

"Okay," Andrew replied, smiling directly at the teacher.

Grace and Sarah, sitting together, giggled softly and whispered to each other.

"Girls! Are you going to disrupt my lesson too?" the teacher barked, pointing Grace to another desk. "And you," pointing at Andrew, "Sit with Sarah."

"With pleasure," Andrew replied with a grin.

Grace, slightly upset by the teacher's punishment, tried to concentrate on the lesson, glancing at Sarah and Andrew from time to time. They seemed engrossed in conversation, paying no attention to the lesson.

At the end of the class, Grace packed her textbooks and overheard Sarah talking to Andrew.

"Hahaha," Sarah laughed. "Come on," she replied enthusiastically.

"Great!" Andrew said cheerfully. "It was nice to meet you," he extended his hand.

"And you," Sarah replied, shaking hands. Andrew left the room, and Grace approached Sarah with a curious smile.

"Oh, come on!" Sarah said, laughing and shoving Grace playfully.

"Tell me everything," Grace insisted cheerfully.

"We'll talk later," Sarah said, looking embarrassed.

After school, during lunch, the friends actively discussed their first day back.

"Yes, it was funny," they laughed together.

"The chemistry teacher is so enthusiastic," Grace mimicked the teacher, "But I still understood nothing."

"Me neither," Sarah giggled, looking away.

"We both know why you didn't understand," Grace teased. "How is he? What did he say? Tell me everything."

"Well, first..."

"Sarah! Here you are!" Andrew interrupted, approaching their table.

"Speak of the devil..." Grace muttered, grinning.

Sarah looked at Andrew and switched her focus. "Hi, how was your day?"

"Mind-bogglingly boring," Andrew sighed dramatically, twirling his pen. "You must be Grace," he said, looking at her.

"That's right, Andrew, isn't it?" Grace asked, glancing at him.

"What?" he asked, distracted.

"Andrew? Is that right?" Grace repeated.

"Oh, yes, that's right!" he smiled, extending his hand.

"Cold..." she thought, shaking his hand.

"Well, it seems that this is for you," he pointed towards a car with a waving woman. "I won't keep you. Have a nice day!" he said and left.

"Thank you!" the girls replied, walking towards the car.

Once in the back seat, the friends cheerfully discussed their day.

"I see the first day of school went well?" Monica remarked.

"Oh, yes," Grace began enthusiastically. "First there was chemistry. We got seated seperately, and it wasn't fair, but it's okay. We also got a lot of homework! Can you imagine? And someone might have a crush!" she teased, glancing at Monica, who kept her eyes on the road.

"I'm not in love," Sarah muttered.

Monica laughed and looked at her daughter. "How was your day?"

"Fine," Sarah replied, staring out the window.

Grace continued to talk animatedly about the day's events.

—⁂—

Arriving home, Monica hurried to the kitchen.

"So much homework on the first day, but are they bullying?! Is it really going to be like this for the whole sixth grade?!" Grace exclaimed, kicking off her shoes in the hallway.

"Oh, yes, yes, it's too much. I agree with you," Sarah replied absently, her eyes distant and dreamy, as if lost in thoughts that danced far from the mundane complaints of school.

The comforting aroma of freshly cooked chicken and potatoes soon filled the house. The lively strains of "Ain't No Mountain High Enough" from the radio provided a backdrop to Monica's cheerful efforts in the kitchen. Monica, slicing vegetables for her signature mozzarella salad, sang along softly, her movements light and rhythmic. Grace watched Sarah's amused expression as she looked at her mother's exaggeratedly animated cooking, their shared laughter creating a fleeting bubble of joy amidst the routine.

"What are you laughing at?" Monica asked with a smile, noticing the girls' mirth. "Run and change, and then help set the table. Dad will be coming home soon," she added, glancing at the wall clock.

At the dinner table, the conversation turned to the first day of school. Sarah animatedly recounted the day's events, including poor Jim's tomato juice mishap. As Sarah reached for the breadbasket, her distracted hand knocked over a crystal glass too close to the edge. The glass shattered on the floor, and sharp shards sliced into Grace's leg. Grace screamed, her voice a mix of surprise and piercing pain.

Sarah's face went pale as she rushed to help, her hands trembling as she tried to remove the shards. In her frantic state, she cut herself, but her concern for Grace overshadowed her own pain. "Oh my God, Grace, I'm so sorry! I didn't mean to! Are you okay?!" she babbled, tears welling up in her eyes.

Monica and William hurried over, their faces etched with concern. Monica, while still exuding care, quickly went to get the first aid kit. William gently lifted Grace into his arms, carrying her to her room as Monica applied disinfectant and bandaged Sarah's hands.

"It's alright, sweetheart," Monica reassured Sarah, her tone soothing but carrying an undercurrent of frustration as she attended to the girl. "It'll heal soon," she added, placing a kiss on Sarah's wound before turning her attention back to Grace.

"William," Monica said, her voice soft but firm, "take Grace to her room. She shouldn't be walking on that leg right now."

William nodded and carried Grace to her room, settling her gently onto the bed. Sarah, still in tears, stood in the doorway. "I'm so sorry, Grace. I never meant for this to happen," she whispered, her voice breaking.

Grace, feeling the sting of both physical pain and emotional distance, gave a tired nod. "It's okay," she murmured, her voice barely audible.

William gave Grace a reassuring smile, saying goodnight and turning off the light. Grace lay in the darkness, her leg throbbing painfully. As the quiet enveloped her, she thought about her mother's comforting presence, her soft touch and gentle voice that used to soothe her.

The contrast with the warmth and concern from Sarah's family only deepened her sense of isolation. The soothing lullaby Monica sang to Sarah only amplified Grace's feelings of longing and loss.

"It hurts so much," Grace thought, tears mingling with the ache. "I miss my mom, her hugs, her smiles. Why does everyone else seem to have what I'm missing?"

Exhausted and overwhelmed, Grace eventually fell into a troubled sleep, her face swollen and aching from the night's events. The next morning, as she looked at her reflection, the image staring back seemed foreign and disheartening. Sarah stood at the door, radiating warmth with her new pearl hairpin and a bright smile, eagerly offering a hug that exuded comfort and affection.

As they walked to school, a dull gray blanket covered the sky. Grace, lost in her thoughts, responded absently to Sarah's cheerful chatter. When Andrew appeared at school, waiting for Sarah, he stood out with his casual confidence. Grace, observing from the sidelines, couldn't help but feel a flutter of something—perhaps it was a budding interest in Andrew. As Sarah and Andrew chatted animatedly, Grace's mood lifted slightly, her thoughts drifting away from the pain and isolation of the past night.

—⁂—

"Everyone wants to be happy, right?!" demanded Grace, her voice tinged with desperation.

"Happiness is a pretty broad concept; everyone has their own idea of it," Sam replied, his voice smooth and almost hypnotic. "For some, happiness is found in routine, while others lose the meaning of life searching for it," he concluded, his eyes glinting with a knowing look.

Grace looked down at her brooding reflection on the polished marble floor, feeling a strange chill despite the warm room.

"What do you want most, Grace?" Sam whispered, leaning forward slightly, his gaze penetrating.

After a moment's thought, Grace replied, "My happiness is peace," she said slowly, meeting Samuel's intense stare. "I don't want to suffer anymore. I don't want to feel guilty. I want to let go of, as you said, 'the demons of my past.'" Abruptly lifting her head, she asked, "Can you help me, Doctor?"

Sam leaned back, a faint, almost imperceptible smile playing on his lips. "Therapy... it's not a snap of the fingers," he said, snapping his fingers for emphasis. "Therapy is a form of self-help. I can guide you on the path, offer options, but I can't encroach on your will. You decide what to do, choose your path, set priorities, Grace. I'm just a mentor," he reasoned philosophically, his tone almost too smooth.

Grace, trying to collect her thoughts, focused on the marigolds in the vase, their bright orange petals seeming out of place in the dimly lit room.

"Earlier, you mentioned that life with Sarah's parents, and with her, became a mistake. Why do you think that?" the doctor asked, his curiosity piqued.

Grace looked up from the vase on the coffee table and began to answer, her voice barely above a whisper. "Living with them was supposed to be a new beginning, but it only reminded me of what I'd lost. They were kind, but I always felt like an outsider, a burden. Sarah tried to include me, but I could see the difference in how they treated her. It was like there was an invisible line I could never cross."

Sam nodded slowly, his fingers steepled under his chin. "It's common to feel like an outsider in a new environment, especially after such a traumatic loss. But the question remains, Grace, what will you do to find your peace?" His eyes seemed to bore into hers, as if searching for something deep within her.

Grace shivered, feeling an inexplicable sense of unease. "I don't know," she admitted. "I just want to stop feeling this way. I want to move on, but I don't know how."

Sam's smile widened ever so slightly. "It's a journey, Grace. Sometimes, to find peace, we have to confront the very things we're running from. Are you ready to face your demons?"

Grace's heart raced at his words. There was something in his tone, something almost predatory, that made her feel like prey. But she pushed the feeling aside and nodded. "I'm ready," she whispered.

"Good," Sam whispered. "Because only by confronting them can you hope to overcome them."

Grace looked at him, a flicker of doubt in her eyes. She sat back in her chair, drawing in a deep breath, trying to steady herself. "So, what's next?" she asked, her voice trembling slightly.

Sam leaned forward, his eyes never leaving hers. "Next, we delve deeper. We explore those dark corners of your mind, the ones you try to avoid. It's going to be difficult, but it's the only way to find the peace you seek."

Grace nodded slowly, feeling a mix of fear and determination. "I'm ready to try," she said, more to herself than to him.

Sam's smile returned, a look of satisfaction crossing his face. "That's the spirit, Grace. We'll make progress, one step at a time."

The room fell silent, the weight of the conversation hanging in the air. Grace felt a sense of foreboding, but also a glimmer of hope. She knew the path ahead would present challenges, but she hoped to find the peace she desperately sought with Sam's guidance.

—ɯ—

"The results of the fourth test leave much to be desired," the chemistry teacher lamented on the last day of school. "But there are also excellent results that still give hope to the class!" she added in a matter-of-fact tone. "Grace! The highest score in the class!"

Grace blinked, genuinely surprised, her eyes widening as she looked down at her desk. She never expected to be singled out.

"Um, Miss," Andrew raised his hand, his pen twirling between his fingers. "There must be some mistake in the calculations," he said with a confident smile.

"There can be no mistakes in my calculations, Andrew," the teacher replied irritably. But noticing the confident fire in the student's eyes, she gave in. "So be it. According to school policy, I have to check your work again." She reviewed the notebook. After a minute of silence, her voice broke the quiet.

"It's amazing. I really did miss something," Miss Florence said in dismay. "In that case, Andrew and Grace have the best results."

Andrew, getting up from his desk, made a mocking low bow in front of the teacher, causing the entire class to burst into laughter. The teacher looked coldly at him from under her glasses.

"Congratulations!" Andrew approached Grace with a playful smile.

Wishing a good Christmas, Miss Florence dismissed the class for the holidays.

At the end of the day, according to tradition, Andrew accompanied the girls to Monica's car, encouraging Sarah, who had received a rather low score on the test.

"Don't worry, there's no point in school for the most part; it's just a stage of life where you're expected to totally submit and completely deny its existence," Andrew joked.

"Hello, girls! Andrew," Sarah's mom greeted the kids.

"Hello!" Andrew replied in a carefree tone. "I apparently have a competitor in knowledge," he said, addressing Grace.

Grace blushed slightly, trying to hide her joy for Sarah's sake, and got into the car. Monica said goodbye to Andrew and started driving home.

"What happened, my daughter? Why are you so sad?" Monica asked with concern.

"I... failed the fourth test..." Sarah said in disappointment.

"It's okay... what about yours, Grace?" Monica asked, her tone noticeably different.

"One hundred out of a hundred," Grace said softly.

Monica nodded approvingly in Grace's direction but spun the radio to defuse the situation. Grace could feel the subtle but ever-present divide—Monica cared, but there was always a slight distance, a reminder that she was not truly her daughter.

When they arrived home, Monica handed the keys to Grace and said, "We'll be back later. Will you open the door? There's food in the fridge. William will be back in two hours, okay?"

"Uh, okay," Grace replied in confusion, not understanding what was going on.

"That's great!" Monica said with slightly feigned enthusiasm. "See you later!"

Grace looked at Sarah, who glanced at her and then turned her gaze out the window. Slightly upset by her friend's reaction and completely surprised by what had happened, Grace closed the door and headed towards the house.

Entering through the front door, Grace took off her backpack, put on her slippers, and went to the kitchen. Opening the refrigerator, she saw her half-eaten breakfast, tomato juice, and a stale salad from last night's dinner. With a sigh, Grace closed the refrigerator and went into the empty hall. The lights were turned off in the entire house; it felt like an endless sleepover where she played the role of a daughter in a family that wasn't truly hers. She sat down on the sofa, turned on the TV, and waited for William.

—◊◊◊—

"Thank you, Dad!" Sarah said happily.

"Eh? What? What time is it?" Grace woke up, having dozed off while watching a comedy show. Wiping her eyes, she noticed it was already nine o'clock in the evening. Hearing Sarah and her parents arriving, she ran to meet them.

"Hi, Grace, aren't you tired?" Monica asked, taking off her jacket.

"Nah, you didn't bring anything by any chance..." Grace began, but Sarah interrupted her friend.

"Look! Beautiful, isn't it?" Sarah showed off her new dress with enthusiasm.

"Beautiful!" William affirmed.

"Yes, it's very beautiful," Grace replied, her surprise tinged with bitterness. "Why did they buy it for you?!" she asked, a bit indignant, remembering that Sarah had failed the test.

"I don't know, but I like it!" Sarah replied joyfully, moving towards the sofa where Grace had been sleeping.

Monica, heading to the kitchen to warm up the food she bought on the way, asked, "How are you, Grace? Did you eat?"

Before Grace could answer, Monica continued, "How was your day at school?"

"I already told you," Grace whispered, sitting down at the table and looking down.

"I must have forgotten. Will you repeat it?" Monica asked as she took out the plates.

"I got the highest score on the test," Grace said indifferently, the pride of her success now feeling hollow.

"Well done!" Monica praised while setting the table. "Dear! Sarah! Everything is ready!" she called to her family.

Grace, who always sat next to Sarah, noticed there were only three plates on the table. She went to get a plate and utensils for herself, feeling a pang of exclusion.

"Are you hungry or something?" Monica asked, surprised. "I left food..."

"Yes, hungry," Grace replied, looking at the reheated Chinese food in the microwave, her frustration mounting.

"I thought you had eaten, and I only took three servings. Do you need to heat something up?" Monica asked.

"Yes," Grace said, her voice barely hiding her irritation.

Sitting at the table, Grace finished her recently warmed, ill-fated omelet, trying to comprehend what was happening. Meanwhile, Sarah, with incredible enthusiasm, recounted to her smiling parents how delicious the dish they had brought home was and thanked them for the gorgeous pink dress.

"Grace, did you hear that?" Sarah drew attention to herself in a joyful tone.

"Huh? No, what is it?" Grace asked, picking dried spinach out of her omelet.

"We're leaving for Hawaii tomorrow! For the entire Christmas holiday!" Sarah shouted, excited by the news.

"What? Is this true?!" Grace asked, looking hopefully at Sarah's parents, feeling a flicker of hope.

"Yes! So pack your things; we have a flight in the morning!" Monica replied.

Sarah jumped up from the table and cheerfully ran up the stairs, calling Grace to follow her.

"Be careful, the last step is slightly sagging," Sarah warned. "But it's okay; Dad will fix it for sure when we get back."

The girls ran to pack their things into a suitcase, their excitement palpable. Meanwhile, the parents went to bed.

Grace followed Sarah up the stairs, her heart heavy. While Sarah chattered excitedly about their trip, Grace couldn't shake the feeling of being an outsider in the family. She longed for the same kind of love and attention that Sarah received so effortlessly.

As they packed, Grace couldn't help but wonder if she would ever truly feel like she belonged. She silently promised herself that she would find her own happiness, even if it meant letting go of the hope that Monica and William would ever see her as anything more than Sarah's friend.

"Grace?" Sarah called in a whisper as she opened the door to Grace's room.

"Yes?" Grace replied, sitting up. "Can't you sleep either?"

"Yeah, I was thinking... do you want us to buy you a dress too? You looked so upset earlier," Sarah offered kindly, her eyes full of concern.

Grace felt a warm glow at her friend's thoughtful gesture. "No, you shouldn't. We'd better get something in Hawaii."

"Come on! Maybe we'll lower the suitcase, and, we'll eat something delicious," Sarah suggested cheerfully.

"With pleasure!" Grace agreed, her stomach growling since dinner.

After closing the suitcase in Sarah's room, the friends lifted it from both sides and dragged it to the stairs.

"Shhh, shhh," Grace hissed, trying not to laugh in excitement for the upcoming trip.

"That's it!" they put the suitcase near the stairs.

"How do we get it down now?" Sarah wondered. "Oh! I know!"

Grace stood with her back to the stairs and explained in a whisper to her friend, "I'll stand on the other side, lift the suitcase slightly... yeah, that's it, and I'll—"

Suddenly, the same sagging step that Sarah had warned about gave way. Grace, unable to keep her balance, tumbled backward down the stairs.

"Grace!!!" Sarah screamed in horror.

"AHHH!!!" Grace's scream echoed through the house as the heavy suitcase crashed down on top of her, pushing her down the stairs.

"What happened?!" Monica and William came running in a panic, their faces white with fear as they saw Grace rolling down the stairs with the suitcase barreling behind her.

"Oh my God!" William exclaimed, rushing down the stairs, fearing the worst.

"Ay, ay! It hurts!! I can't move!" Grace cried out, the pain mercilessly surging through her entire body.

Monica, her face stricken with worry, helped William carefully lift the suitcase off Grace and carry her to the car.

At the hospital, the doctor reported that Grace had a concussion and a small crack in two ribs.

"But we're going, aren't we?" Grace asked in a trembling voice, looking hopefully at her parents despite her injuries.

The doctor sternly advised, "I do not recommend that you fly for the next two weeks."

"No..." Grace lay in the hospital bed, blinking in confusion and disappointment, tears welling up in her eyes as the reality of missing the trip sank in.

CHAPTER

4

In the morning, Grace said goodbye to Sarah and her parents, wishing them a pleasant flight.

"I'll miss you!" Sarah said, her voice tinged with genuine affection as she hugged Grace tightly, careful not to press too hard against her friend's bruised ribs.

"Me too," Grace replied, her words heavy with sadness as she held her friend close, wincing slightly as the hug pressed against her sore body. A familiar tightness gripped her chest, a subtle reminder of the anxiety that had taken root since her parents' death, compounded now by the physical pain from her recent fall.

After closing the door behind them, Grace was left alone in the large, empty house. The silence felt oppressive, echoing through the spacious rooms and amplifying the emptiness within her. Sarah's parents had left her money for food and other expenses, a gesture that felt both generous and isolating. Ignoring the untouched food from the previous day, she ordered a pizza and settled in to watch television. The screen flickered through various images, each scene a blur of colors and sounds that failed to capture her attention. Her mind was elsewhere, lost in the past.

Days passed slowly, each one blending into the next in a monotonous blur. The melancholic, seemingly endless loneliness settled deep within her soul, a heavy weight pressing down on her. She wandered through the house aimlessly, her mind a storm of thoughts—about herself, school, and her parents. Inevitably, all her thoughts led back to memories of her late mother, triggering pangs of sorrow and guilt. Monica and William cared for her, but it wasn't the same. Their kindness, while appreciated, could never fill the void left by her parents. It felt like it wasn't enough, no matter how ungrateful it might sound. She felt the lack of what once was each time sadness and worry took hold of her heart, in moments when she wanted to cry, feel sorrow, or laugh. No one could hug Grace the way Lillian had. No one could calm her the way Richard did. The weight of her trauma made it hard to breathe and nights came where she fell asleep with tears in her eyes, the darkness of her room matching the darkness in her heart.

On Christmas Eve, snow fell gently, blanketing the world in a soft, white layer. The air carried a crisp, clean scent, and the first snowflakes danced in the air, creating a magical atmosphere as if the entire world was coming alive and transforming. The sight of the snow brought a small, bittersweet smile to her lips, reminding her of better days. Yet, the joy was always fleeting, overshadowed by the ache of loss that never quite left her.

Waking up, Grace rushed to check the mail, her heart pounding with anticipation. Each step sent a dull ache through her body, a reminder of her recent fall. Within moments, she was holding a postcard from her friend, featuring a photo from Hawaii. Sarah was on the beach, holding a coconut with a colorful umbrella, flanked by Monica and William in Hawaiian shirts. The back of the postcard read: "See you tomorrow!" Grace stared at the picture, a mix of happiness for her friend and a pang of envy gnawing at her heart. Her stomach twisted with a familiar anxiety as she thought of their return. She went outside, needing the fresh air to clear her mind.

Donning a pale blue scarf and warm mittens, Grace headed to the city center, where all the locals were gathering for the annual event— "Decorating the Christmas Tree." The effort of bundling up aggravated the fresh scars on her knees from the crystal shards, making her wince as she adjusted her clothing. The streets were alive with the sound of laughter and festive music, the cold air filled with smelling pine and hot cocoa. She walked among the crowd, feeling both a part of and apart from the joyful throng. As she watched the children decorating the tree, a sense of longing filled her, wishing she could feel the same unbridled joy. The festive atmosphere only deepened her sense of isolation, a stark contrast to the warmth and connection she craved but couldn't quite grasp.

—⁂—

Her feet slipped slightly on the icy road, the chill nipping at her exposed skin. Grace walked slowly, eyes wide with wonder as she took in the New Year's decorations. This year, the locals had outdone themselves. Bright garlands and ornaments illuminated the buildings, casting a warm, inviting glow. Christmas decorations and candy canes hung everywhere, transforming the town into a winter wonderland straight out of a fairy tale.

Among the countless people milling about, her gaze fell on a familiar face in a red hat weaving through the crowd. Her heart skipped a beat.

"Andrew?!"

"Hey?!" the boy responded distractedly, not immediately recognizing the voice calling out to him. After a moment, his eyes lit up with recognition. "Hey! How's it going? How's Sarah?"

"I'm..." Grace felt a flutter of nervousness in her stomach as she spoke. "Good! Sarah's great; they went to Hawaii, so they're having a blast!" She forced a smile, trying to hide the envy and sadness that tugged at her heart.

"Hmm, why didn't you go?" Andrew asked, his curiosity evident.

"I got injured, and I can't fly for a while," she replied, brushing her fingers over her ribs where the bruises from her fall still ached.

"Ah, well, that's okay!" Andrew waved his hand dismissively, his concern shining through. "Is everything alright now?"

"Yes, it's all right now..." Grace said, feeling a bit embarrassed by the attention.

"That's the main thing!" Andrew smiled warmly, then reached out eagerly. "Let's go!" He took Grace's hand, the touch sending a rush of warmth through her despite the cold.

"Wait!" Grace struggled to keep up with his pace, her heart racing not just from the exertion but from being so close to him.

They escaped the whirlwind of strangers, and her eyes fell on a gigantic Christmas tree, towering higher than a three-story building, completely adorned with garlands, tinsel, colorful ornaments, and delicate baubles. The sight was breathtaking, almost magical.

Nearby, a little girl was hanging a porcelain angel on the tree. The sweet aroma of hot chocolate wafted through the air, coming from a nearby stand where they made the most delicious hot chocolate.

"Shall we hang some garlands?" Andrew's voice, full of enthusiasm, suddenly sounded beside her.

"Sure," Grace said, still enchanted by the holiday magic. She took some glowing baubles, and the pair carefully hung them in a circle. After a few minutes, they stepped back to admire their handiwork.

"High five!" Andrew said, grinning, and they exchanged a playful slap of hands.

"Hot chocolate?" Andrew offered the shivering Grace.

"Thank you," she said, smiling softly as she took the aromatic chocolate, the warmth seeping through the cup into her chilled fingers.

Andrew, shaking his head from side to side, suggested taking a walk along the waterfront. "Beautiful tree, isn't it?"

"Very!" Grace responded, her voice lively with excitement.

"There's a waterfront close to here. The city has put up a bunch of other decorations there. Want to check it out?"

"With pleasure!"

After a long and cozy walk, filled with bright decorations, children's laughter, and Andrew's silly jokes, Grace sat on the nearest bench, gazing at the setting sun. The colors of the sunset painted the sky in hues of pink and gold, casting a soft glow over the snow-covered landscape.

"Andrew, have you ever thought about the future?" she asked, her voice quiet and contemplative.

Sitting next to Grace and putting his hands in his pockets, the boy replied, "Honestly, I do not know how my life will turn out," he sighed, closing his eyes.

"You, Andrew? Don't know how your life will turn out?" Grace smirked, raising an eyebrow in playful disbelief.

"I'd like to be a singer, record my album, perform on stage, gather crowds at my huge concerts, sign autographs, and do what artists do," Andrew said dreamily. "But in reality, that plan is too vague. My future is uncertain. Maybe in higher classes, I'll figure it out, but right now... I don't know." he looked at Grace with a certain intensity. "And you?"

"I..." after a brief pause, she continued, "I'd probably become... an astronaut!" she said jokingly, the first thing that came to mind.

They both burst into laughter, but Andrew continued to insist on a serious answer.

"But seriously, what do you see yourself doing when you grow up?"

"My mom used to tell me about plants, and I loved flowers the most," Grace replied. "But the idea of being a gardener doesn't appeal to me. Maybe when I have a house, I'll start planting different flowers in my yard," she sighed dreamily.

"Hmm, that's not a very profitable occupation," Andrew pondered. "You could open a flower shop and sell what you love to other people, sharing the beauty of your flowers with the world. I think Greece would be a great option for you."

"You think? That's a good idea," Grace agreed, feeling a warmth in her chest from his encouragement. "Can I ask you a question?" she began hesitantly.

"Of course!" Andrew replied.

"Do you... like Sarah?" she asked, her voice barely above a whisper, her cheeks flushing with embarrassment.

"What?! No!" he exclaimed, laughing. "We're just good friends from sitting next to each other in the most boring class at school!"

"And that tape she gave you at the beginning of school?" Grace asked, her curiosity piqued.

"I collect old movies; it's my hobby," Andrew answered.

"I see..."

The awkward atmosphere disappeared, and Grace, relaxing, laughed, with Andrew joining in. Once they calmed down, their gazes locked, and their smiles faded. Grace looked softly at Andrew, who responded in kind. For the first time in a long time, the feeling of emptiness, loneliness, and guilt disappeared. Her soul felt warm from the tender gaze of his brown eyes. She moved closer to Andrew's face, closing her eyes slightly. Their lips brushed together in a gentle kiss.

"Your lips are so cold," Grace whispered softly.

"In my defense, it's freezing outside and snowing!" Andrew said cheerfully, reaching for a second kiss.

As he brushed away a strand of hair covering Grace's scar, his fingers grazed her skin, and her thoughts immediately spiraled back to her parents and the car accident. The sudden rush of memories was overwhelming.

"Stop!" Grace suddenly pushed Andrew away and turned, closing her eyes tightly.

"What's wrong?" Andrew asked, his voice tinged with concern.

"It's okay, I just can't…" Grace replied, her voice trembling. "I need to go…"

"Let me walk you," Andrew offered, slightly confused by the sudden change in her mood.

"Okay," Grace said, taking a deep breath to calm herself.

The pair headed towards her home, enjoying the Christmas lights along the way. As they walked, Grace could feel the bruises on her ribs with each step, a reminder of her recent fall. Despite the pain, she hugged Andrew tightly, finding comfort in his presence.

When they reached her house, Grace took out her keys and opened the door, then looked back at Andrew.

"How are you getting home?" she asked anxiously.

"I'll walk, don't worry."

"It's late already. Aren't your parents looking for you?" Grace asked, her concern growing. Andrew's expression dimmed. He looked around thoughtfully and, after a moment, replied.

"Grace…" with a slight pause, he said her name, "I haven't told anyone about this, so I ask you to keep it to yourself as well," taking another pause, he exhaled and said, "I'm an orphan. No one is looking for me." He looked at her trustingly, waiting for her reaction.

Surprise and then understanding reflected on her face. She calmly approached him and gently hugged him. The bitterness of loss and a desire to help resonated in her heart. As she hugged him, the sharp pain from her bruised ribs flared up, but she held on tightly, wanting to be there for him.

"It's okay. It's not a big deal. I'm used to it already. I didn't really know them," Andrew said, brushing off the sympathy.

"I…" Grace, taking a slight pause, decided not to tell Andrew about her own loss, "I'm really sorry." she hugged him again, her voice steady despite the ache in her ribs.

"Thank you," he breathed. "Good night, Grace."

"And you too," she replied, her heart feeling lighter despite the lingering sadness.

—⁂—

Grace entered the house, her footsteps echoing in the silent hall. She leaned heavily against the door, trying to shake off the chill of the evening, but her mind was still buzzing with the warmth of the day. The joy she felt from her walk with Andrew lingered, yet it was tinged with an underlying sadness that she couldn't quite shake.

She made her way to her room, the book about flowers—one that Lilian used to read to her—clutched tightly in her hands. The book felt like a tangible connection to her mother, a bridge to the past that she desperately needed.

"Hi, Mom!" she said, her voice breaking with an excitement she could barely contain as she opened the book. Her smile was radiant, and her eyes sparkled with the afterglow of a day that had been both magical and bittersweet. "You won't believe what happened today!" Her heart raced as she recounted her experience.

Grace settled into her favorite chair, the book resting gently on her lap as if it were a precious artifact. She looked at the pages with a mixture of reverence and nostalgia. "Remember I told you about Andrew? Well, today we spent the whole day together. He doesn't like Sarah—he explained everything to me, including that tape. And we went for a walk, and he bought me the most delicious hot chocolate. I laughed so much, my sides still hurt!" Her voice was filled with genuine joy, each word a reflection of the happiness she had felt.

The glow in her eyes intensified as she continued. "And, Mom, I had my first kiss today! It was... it was amazing and a little strange, but really wonderful. I never thought I'd feel this way, but Andrew was so kind and caring. For the first time, a boy really showed he cared about me. I felt so special, so loved," she said, her voice softening with a mix of joy and longing.

Grace paused, her smile faltering as she looked down at the book. "Sarah is coming back tomorrow. She'll tell me about her adventures in Hawaii. I hope she had a fantastic time," she said, a hint of envy in her voice, but it quickly shifted to something more somber. "My ribs don't hurt as much now. I think they'd have healed faster if you were here," she admitted, her tone laden with sadness.

Her face contorted with grief as she continued, "I miss you so much. I miss Dad too. I want to hug you both, to hear your voices, to have you brush my hair, and for Dad to carry me on his back. I want to feel your love again. It's so hard without you." Her voice cracked, the weight of her emotions almost too heavy to bear. "I love you so much. Why aren't you here with me? Did I do something wrong? Is this my fault? I should have warned Dad about that car. Why is everything so unfair? I'm just a kid! Who should I blame for your deaths? Me? Monica and William gave me a home and food, but they're not you."

She sobbed, her body shaking with the intensity of her grief. "Oh, what am I doing?! Talking to a book like it's a person! I feel so lost and foolish. If only I could go back and tell Dad about that car. If only I hadn't been in such a hurry!" she cried out, her words a mix of anguish and regret.

Grace threw the book away from her, her frustration and sorrow overwhelming. She curled up in her chair, her tears drying on her cheeks as exhaustion took over. Despite the small victories of the day, the emptiness and grief were still raw, leaving her to drift into a restless sleep, the weight of her emotions hanging heavy in the room.

"Grace?" a familiar voice whispered softly, cutting through the haze of her dreams. Grace struggled to open her eyes, and her heart leaped when she recognized Sarah's figure sitting on her bed.

"Sarah!" she exclaimed, throwing herself into her friend's arms. "You're so tanned! How was it? How was the flight? Tell me everything!" Her voice bubbled with excitement and curiosity, her earlier sadness momentarily forgotten.

The friends spent the entire morning nestled in bed, sharing stories and laughter about Sarah's Hawaiian adventure. Sarah recounted her "grand stories" with animated gestures and enthusiasm, while Grace listened with rapt attention, her mind painting vivid pictures of the exotic locales and experiences.

"Girls! The food is ready!" Monica's voice called from the kitchen, breaking the cozy bubble they had created.

"We'll be right there!" Sarah replied, glancing at Grace with a playful smile.

As they prepared to leave the comfort of the bed, Grace couldn't help but tease her friend. "But your tan is amazing," she said with a sly grin. "Jamie will definitely appreciate it!"

"Ugh! No way," Sarah replied with a dramatic grimace, but her eyes sparkled with amusement. "By the way, speaking of boys," she began casually, her tone nonchalant but her eyes alight with excitement, "It seems I like Andrew. Look at what he sent me!" She pulled out a delicate heart-shaped pendant, its sparkle catching the light.

Grace's smile faltered as she took in the pendant. "But we... Does he really like Sarah, after all?" she wondered silently, her thoughts a tangled mess of confusion and heartache. Despite the pang of jealousy and uncertainty that tugged at her, she saw how happy Sarah looked and couldn't bring herself to spoil the moment.

"But I'll tell you more later. Let's go eat!" Sarah urged with a bright smile, clearly eager to move on from their chat and enjoy the meal.

Grace, her mind swirling with mixed emotions, followed Sarah out of the room. She kept her silence, to hold back the memories of her bittersweet evening with Andrew. For now, she would stay quiet, allowing Sarah's joy to shine through.

She chose to remain silent, keeping her feelings and thoughts hidden. The confusion of the previous night lingered, but Grace resolved to keep her emotions in check, at least until the right moment. For now, she would focus on her friend's happiness, preserving the delicate balance of their friendship.

—⁓—

"So Andrew likes Sarah, or you?" Sam asked, his voice smooth and measured, but with an underlying edge that hinted at something more. "It's a bit more complicated than that," Grace replied, her voice trembling slightly. "I often didn't fully understand what was happening myself."

Sam leaned back in his chair, his eyes gleaming with an inscrutable intensity. The sharp, almost calculating focus of his gaze contrasted his calm demeanor.

"And what were your feelings towards Andrew?"And what were your feelings towards Andrew?" The doctor's relaxed posture contrasted with his penetrating curiosity, which both comforted and unsettled Grace.

Grace hesitated, her eyes drifting to the vase on the table, a rare moment of distraction. She seemed to search for the right words, her fingers fidgeting with the hem of her sleeve.

"I felt…" Grace began, her voice catching as she looked up. "Andrew was nice," she drawled, her expression softening as she spoke. "Funny," she added with a wistful laugh that barely masked her lingering sadness. "Sweet and caring."

Sam's lips curled into a faint, enigmatic smile, his eyes never leaving Grace's face. "So, did you like him?" he asked, his tone gently probing, yet laced with an undertone of something more ominous.

"I don't know," Grace sighed deeply, her shoulders drooping as if the weight of her memories was too much to bear. "Maybe I had romantic feelings, or maybe it was just that he understood me—he knew what it was like to feel lonely…"

Sam's eyes narrowed slightly, his expression inscrutable. He leaned forward, his gaze intense and unwavering. "And Sarah? What happened between them? Are they still together? Do you feel regret?" The questions came quickly, each one delivered with a cold, clinical precision that made Grace shiver.

"I don't know," Grace said dismissively, her voice wavering. The flicker of distress in her eyes was visible as she tried to avoid Sam's unyielding stare.

"Why do you refer to the situation with the three of you as a mistake? And how did you end up with the Freemans? I'm sorry for the abrupt questions, but they need answers," Sam continued, his tone unchanging but his eyes glinting with an almost predatory curiosity.

Grace's eyes fell to the floor, her fingers gripping the armrests of the chair as if they were the only things anchoring her at the moment. She took a deep breath, her voice trembling as she spoke.

"It all started at graduation," Grace began, her voice soft but steady. "After graduation, I was placed with new guardians, and I lost touch with Andrew and Sarah. Everything changed so quickly, and I never really got a chance to process it all…"

Sam's gaze remained fixed on her, a subtle smirk playing at the corners of his mouth. His demeanor, while outwardly professional, carried a chilling hint of satisfaction, as though he were savoring the unspoken truths behind her words. Grace felt a shiver run down her spine as she met his gaze, unable to fully shake the unsettling feeling that lingered in the room.

—⚎—

"So Grace, maybe we should dance?" James asked, noticing Grace's distant expression as she watched Sarah and Andrew dance.

"Pass," Grace replied curtly, her voice betraying her irritation.

"Suit yourself. I'm heading to the punch bowl," James said with a shrug and walked off.

Grace rolled her eyes and turned her attention back to Sarah and Andrew. The sight of them together only deepened her sense of isolation. Over the years, Grace's relationship with Sarah had become strained. What had once been a close friendship had dissolved into a series of misunderstandings and silent resentments. Grace often felt like an outsider in her own life, overshadowed by Sarah's ease and the attention she received.

The events leading up to the prom had only exacerbated these feelings. Sarah had received praise and attention effortlessly, while Grace felt relegated to the background. Even as they prepared for the evening, it was clear who was the center of attention. Grace's sense of displacement was palpable, her frustration simmering just below the surface.

"What the hell?" Grace exclaimed as she saw James dancing with another girl. Annoyance and a touch of jealousy colored her voice.

"You didn't want to dance," James said, puzzled by her reaction.

"Do whatever you want," Grace said dismissively, her eyes shifting to the punch bowl. The sight of James with someone else was just another irritation in a night filled with them.

She grabbed a glass of fruit punch, clearly spiked with something stronger, and made her way towards the exit. The evening had become a stage for her unresolved emotions and hidden frustrations.

Sarah noticed Grace leaving and hurried over to Andrew.

"Oh, damn it!" Sarah said, fumbling for her phone as it rang incessantly. "Go ahead, I'll catch up later. Mom is calling again—how many times?!"

"Okay," Andrew agreed, letting Sarah deal with the call.

Grace leaned against the railing, her gaze fixed on the river below. Her thoughts were a whirlpool of confusion and bitterness.

"How are you?" Andrew asked as he joined her on the stairs.

"Perfectly," Grace said coldly, not meeting his eyes. "James went off to dance with someone else, and I'm here, drinking... whatever this is," she said, lifting her glass.

Andrew chuckled and took out a flask from his jacket, handing it to her with a teasing smile.

"You'll definitely know what it is," he said.

"Thanks," Grace said, taking a gulp. "Ugh! What is this?" she grimaced.

"Apple juice," Andrew replied with a smirk.

Their laughter was a fleeting escape from the heaviness Grace felt. She tried to shift the conversation to something lighter.

"Have you applied to college yet?" Grace asked.

"What? Is that how you want to spend graduation night?" Andrew raised an eyebrow, amused.

"Well, we could discuss your stellar performance on stage," Grace teased.

"Haha, no thanks. So, um, how are you really?"

Grace sighed deeply, her eyes reflecting the turmoil inside.

"Honestly, it feels like I'm always heading somewhere, but I don't know where or why. Everything seems pointless," she admitted, her voice tinged with frustration.

Andrew's expression grew thoughtful.

"My father used to say, 'Even when passing through the darkest valley, a person should not fear its darkness,'" he said, glancing down. He rolled up his sleeve, revealing a scar on his forearm—a burn mark from a cigarette.

"What does that mean?" Grace asked, searching his face for answers.

"I... don't really know. Mostly, he was a jerk," Andrew said, his smile bitter.

Grace noticed the scar and felt a pang of empathy.

"I need to tell you something," she said firmly. "William and Monica, Sarah's parents—they're not my actual parents."

"But you're like sisters," Andrew said, confused.

"We were friends before," Grace explained. "My parents died when I was 12. Sarah's parents adopted me. They care for me, but it's not the same. I never really felt like I belonged. Sometimes I feel like a guest in my own life," Grace said, placing a comforting hand on Andrew's cheek.

"And this scar?" Andrew asked, understanding dawning in his eyes.

"Yes," Grace said softly.

Andrew embraced her, offering comfort. Grace clung to him, tears slipping down her cheeks.

"Do you remember that Christmas night?" Andrew asked gently.

"Yes," Grace said, rubbing her eyes, feeling an unusual closeness with him.

The moment was tender, their faces inches apart. As they leaned in for what seemed like a kiss, Sarah's voice cut through the night air.

"What the hell?!" Sarah shouted, her tone a mix of surprise and indignation. Andrew jolted up, looking alarmed.

"Wait here!" Grace said, her heart racing as she hurried after Sarah, leaving Andrew behind. The kiss that almost happened lingered in the air, unfulfilled and unresolved.

Sarah slammed the door with a deafening bang, the sound echoing through the empty school hallway. Her anger was palpable as she stormed away, her footsteps echoing sharply against the linoleum floor. Grace, determined and visibly shaken, chased after her.

"Do you want to take my boyfriend now?!" Sarah's voice, harsh and piercing, cut through the stillness. She whirled around, her eyes blazing with fury.

"There was nothing! Calm down!" Grace's voice quivered with desperation as she tried to defend herself. "Andrew just hugged me, and that's it!"

"That's how I'm supposed to believe it?! Disbelief and rage dripped from Sarah's voice. She jabbed her finger towards the narrow gap between their faces. "Your faces were two fucking centimeters apart!" Her anger was a visible storm, her face flushed and her breaths coming in ragged bursts. "I saw how you looked at us at the party. Even if nothing happened, you wanted something to happen, didn't you?!"

"Yes, how do you know?!" Grace's frustration erupted as she shouted back, her eyes wet with unshed tears. "Yes, I wanted to! This was the first time I did something for myself!" Her voice broke with the weight of her emotions.

"For all this time?!" Sarah's voice was bitter, her words cutting like a knife. "You've been screwing up my life! Every Christmas, you cried and ruined the holiday for everyone! Whenever I fought with my mom, instead of being there for me, you'd wallow in your self-pity! And now, you have the nerve to act like you've been wronged? My parents took you in, and all you've done is make everything about your own insecurities!"

"How can you say that?!" Grace's face turned red with a mix of anger and betrayal. "Whenever you were upset, Monica comforted you! I got leftovers for the holidays while you were off to Hawaii or wherever, leaving me behind! I was treated like a stranger in my own home! You think I ruined your life? You're living my dream! You have a family, love, gifts—everything I never had!"

"Oh, so I'm the ungrateful one?!" Sarah's voice was a mix of rage and hurt. Her hands trembled as she spoke. "Poor little Grace, always the victim!"

Suddenly, Sarah's face contorted in pain. She clutched her stomach, her complexion draining of color, and she collapsed to her knees, heaving violently. The contents of her stomach spilled onto the floor, a stark contrast against the polished tiles.

"Oh my God! Are you all right?" Grace's panic was evident as she rushed to her sister's side, her hands shaking as she reached out.

"Don't come near me!" Sarah's voice was hoarse and filled with anger as she shoved Grace away. "It's okay! Just stay away!" Her eyes were wild with distress, her body trembling uncontrollably.

"People don't just throw up on the floor!Grace's voice carried a tinge of desperation and fear. She paced, her hands wringing together, her face pale with concern.

Sarah leaned heavily against a nearby locker, her face streaked with tears and smeared makeup. Pain and revelation wracked Sarah's sobs.

"I'm pregnant..." she finally managed, her voice breaking into a sob.

"What?!" Grace's eyes widened in shock and her breath caught in her throat. "When were you planning to tell me? Does Andrew know?"

"No," Sarah's mascara smeared across her cheeks, her face a mask of anguish.

"Let me help..." Grace's voice was soft, pleading, as she tried to bridge the chasm that had opened between them.

"No!" Sarah's voice was a raw scream, filled with agony and resentment. "Get out! You've ruined enough already! We clearly see our past differently," she hissed, her eyes blazing with anger and hurt. "Just leave before you make things worse!"

Grace stood there for a moment, her heart aching and her body trembling. The hurt and anger from the confrontation weighed heavily on her. With a heavy sigh, she turned and walked away, her shoulders slumped and her steps echoing through the empty hall.

"Sarah!" Andrew's voice called out anxiously as he hurried towards the scene, his expression a mix of concern and confusion.

Grace ignored Andrew completely, her gaze fixed ahead, her mind numb from the confrontation.

At home, Grace's movements were swift and frantic as she packed her belongings into a suitcase. Her hands shook as she threw clothes into the bag, her heart pounding with a mixture of sadness and resolve. She glanced around the room one last time, a sense of finality hanging in the air. With a heavy heart, she left the house, never to return.

CHAPTER

5

Life felt completely different.

The early morning fog enveloped the city like a shroud, casting everything in a muted, gray light. Grace sat alone on a bench, the cold biting through her thin coat and numbing her skin. The chill seemed to seep into her very bones. Her breath misted in the frosty air as she hugged herself tightly, trying to ward off the cold. The memories of New Year's Eve walks with Andrew—the warmth of his hand in hers, his laughter echoing through the crisp night—seemed like a distant dream, their warmth starkly contrasted by the icy reality around her.

She felt completely adrift, overwhelmed by the disorienting mix of her recent losses and the dismal morning. The reality of what she had done—leaving Sarah, the confrontation, and walking away from everything familiar—seemed too vast to comprehend. She felt lost in a sea of regret and confusion, her emotions intertwined with sorrow and bitterness.

"Excuse me... Ma'am," a voice cut through her fog of despair.

Startled, Grace's eyes flew open. The blinding sunlight pierced through the morning mist, making her squint against its harsh glare. The city's noise—distant sirens, the chatter of pedestrians, the murmur of distant conversations—felt like a surreal backdrop to her predicament. A policeman stood before her, his uniform crisp and his badge glinting ominously. The contrast between his pristine appearance and her disheveled state made her feel even more isolated.

"Ma'am," the officer repeated, his tone firm but not unkind. "Are you a high school graduate?"

Grace's heart raced as she struggled to sit up, her movements stiff from the cold. Her mind was a whirlwind of panic and confusion. Her eyes, still puffy from lack of sleep, met his with a mixture of alarm and helplessness.

"Yes," she replied, her voice a thin whisper.

The policeman's gaze softened slightly, though his posture remained authoritative. "Alright then, let's go to the station. We'll sort this out."

Grace's panic surged. "No, no, no," she stammered, her voice rising in a shaky panic. She fumbled with her backpack, her hands cold and unsteady. Her heart pounded furiously, each beat a loud reminder of her fear. She made a clumsy attempt to get up, but her movements were awkward and disoriented. The officer gently but firmly placed a hand on her shoulder, grounding her in the reality of her situation.

In the sterile, dimly lit room of the police station, the reality of her situation hit her hard. The fluorescent lights flickered overhead, their harsh illumination making the walls feel like they were closing in on her. The air was thick with the smell of disinfectant and old coffee, and the quiet hum of distant conversations only amplified her sense of isolation. Grace sat on a hard plastic chair, her hands trembling uncontrollably as she tried to steady her breathing.

"This can't be happening," she thought frantically. Her mind raced with fears and worst-case scenarios. She had never been in trouble before—never had a reason to be at a police station. The unfamiliar setting only intensified her sense of dread. The enormity of the situation seemed to press down on her, each second feeling like an eternity. "What if they think I'm a troublemaker? What if they won't let me go?"

Her thoughts swirled chaotically as she glanced nervously around the room. The officer sitting across from her, a woman with a weary, indifferent demeanor, seemed to add to her growing sense of dread. The officer's monotone voice and impassive gaze felt like a cold barrier, and Grace's anxiety only heightened as she struggled to make sense of the situation.

"Name, surname, age?" the officer asked, her voice carrying a tone of detached routine.

"Grace Bailey," Grace replied, her voice barely above a whisper. She clasped her cold, sweaty hands together, trying to quell the trembling.

The officer's pen hovered above the form, and her eyes, though tired, showed a flicker of interest. "Bailey... with an 'e'?"

"Yes, with an 'e'," Grace said quickly, her attempt at a reassuring smile faltering. Her mind raced with mounting fears. Why had she given her real name? What if this led to something worse? Her heart raced with a panic she had never known before.

"Age?" the officer continued, her tone still flat.

"Seventeen," Grace said, her voice trembling. The fear that gripped her made it hard to think clearly, and the sterile, unfeeling environment of the station seemed to amplify her distress.

The officer looked up for the first time, her gaze impassive. "Hmm, a minor and already causing trouble," she said with a hint of disdain. "Parents' number?"

Grace's heart sank as she tried to recall Monica and William's contact information. She had rarely spoken to Tom outside of family gatherings, and now she was relying on him in a moment of crisis. Calling Sarah's parents wasn't an option. The last thing she wanted was to see yet another difference between her and Sarah. The weight of the situation made her feel even more isolated.

"I have a right for one call, right?" Grace said anxiously. "May I use it?"

"Sure…" the woman, irritably, closed the documents and exited the room with the girl.

With shaking hands, she dialed Tom's number, the phone's beeps echoing ominously in the silence. Each ring seemed to stretch into eternity, amplifying her anxiety. The tired-looking officer glanced at her occasionally, her gaze indifferent, adding to Grace's growing sense of desperation.

The phone finally picked up, and Tom's voice came through a mix of concern and confusion. "Hello?"

"Tom, it's Grace. I'm in a bit of trouble. Can you come pick me up?" Grace's voice was a mix of relief and anxiety. She could barely believe she was asking for help from someone she rarely spoke to.

"What kind of trouble? Are you okay?" Tom's concern was clear, but Grace could hear the uncertainty in his voice.

"I'm at the station. I did nothing serious, just fell asleep on a bench. It's a long story," Grace explained awkwardly, her eyes darting around the room.

"And Monica and William? Are they alright? Why can't they come get you?" Tom asked, his worry palpable.

"They're fine. I had a fight with Sarah. Can you pick me up?" Grace's voice was a desperate plea.

"Alright, don't worry. I'll be there soon," Tom reassured her.

Grace thanked him, her heart still pounding as she hung up. She sank back into her chair, her mind a tumultuous sea of fear and relief. The minutes ticked by slowly, each second stretching into an agonizing wait.

She closed her eyes, trying to steady her breathing and calm the storm of emotions roiling within her.

—⚬—

"Well," Tom said, gesturing towards the apartment with a welcoming sweep of his hand. "Make yourself at home."

"Thank you," Grace replied softly, her voice tinged with exhaustion and relief. "And where is your bathroom?"

"Right down the hall. I'll call William, let him know you're with us," Tom said, picking up the phone.

Grace walked down the hallway, her footsteps light against the polished wooden floor. As she moved, the subtle hum of the city outside grew quieter, replaced by the comforting sounds of home. She soon reached the bathroom, where the soft, warm light created a soothing atmosphere. The cool tiles felt refreshing beneath her feet as she washed her face, trying to shake off the lingering unease from the day's events.

"Grace!" Julia's voice rang out, filled with surprise and warmth. "How you've grown up! Such a beauty!"

In the kitchen, a middle-aged woman stood with a dish towel in hand. Her dark hair had a slight disheveled look, but her eyes sparkled with genuine affection. She stepped forward and enveloped Grace in a tight hug, her embrace a comforting reminder of family.

"How are you?" Julia asked, her voice laced with concern.

"I'm alright," Grace replied, her eyes glistening. "Aren't you hungry? Do you want to eat?"

"Of course!" Julia said with a smile. "I'd hate for you to go hungry. It's been a hectic day, and I was just about to start dinner."

As Julia hurried back to the stove, Grace couldn't help but notice the comforting aroma of home-cooked food wafting through the air. The smell was a stark contrast to the cold, sterile environment of the police station. It brought with it a sense of warmth and safety that Grace had desperately missed.

The family gathered around the table, their laughter and chatter filling the room. Tom shared stories about Richard, Grace's father, and the nostalgia in his voice was palpable.

"I remember picking Richard up from the prom," Tom said, his eyes twinkling with fond remembrance. "He got into an argument with another guy, and it twisted into a full-blown fight. The police were called, and, of course, his older brother came to the rescue. That rascal, Richard."

Grace listened intently, a wistful smile on her lips. The stories were a bittersweet reminder of the father she had lost. Each story brought Richard's youth to life, filling her heart with nostalgia.

"You look a lot like him," Tom said, his gaze lingering on Grace with a mix of sadness and pride. "Richard had that same fiery spirit."

"Really?" Grace asked, her voice barely above a whisper. She couldn't quite believe how much of her father was still visible to her.

"Oh yes," Julia chimed in, picking up where Tom had left off. "Richard was quite the troublemaker. Always up to something that kept us on our toes."

Tom continued, his voice filled with laughter. "Oh, there was this one time in school when Richard was about 14 or 15. He almost got expelled for his antics. He flirted with his biology teacher and set off firecrackers in the classroom. The teacher was so startled she fell off her chair."

"How did the firecrackers stay lit for so long?" Grace laughed, her eyes bright with amusement. It was moments like these that made her feel closer to her father, as if these shared stories briefly bridged the distance between them.

"Ah, we had a trick," Tom said, leaning in with a conspiratorial grin. "We'd use candy wrappers or plasticine to delay the detonation, and wax to keep the smoke down."

Grace laughed heartily, the sound ringing with genuine joy. The warmth of the room, the delicious meal, and the shared laughter provided a soothing balm to her troubled heart. The sense of belonging, the feeling of being surrounded by family, was a rare and precious comfort that she had yearned for.

As the evening wore on, Grace felt a profound sense of peace settling over her. Grace gently set aside the chaos of her day, replacing it with the calm and warmth of being with loved ones. The comforting presence of Tom and Julia, the shared stories about her father, and the simple pleasure of a home-cooked meal all combined to create a sanctuary of solace.

Grace's heart, once heavy with worry and grief, now felt lighter. The familial bond and the fond memories of her father provided a soothing counterpoint to the turmoil she had faced. It was as if the world outside had faded away, leaving only the comforting embrace of family and the enduring legacy of her father's spirit.

"Can I stay with you until classes start?" Grace asked, her eyes hopeful.

"Of course! Stay as long as you want," Julia replied enthusiastically. "You are always welcome here."

"Thank you," Grace said, her voice filled with genuine gratitude.

The day had transformed from a source of anxiety into a haven of warmth and connection, and Grace felt a profound sense of peace, knowing that, even in her darkest moments, she had a place where she truly belonged.

—ɯ—

"The Freemans are my uncle and aunt on my dad's side," Grace clarified, her voice soft and hesitant. "After a quarrel with Sarah and feeling abandoned in her family, I couldn't go back there," she continued, her gaze falling to the floor.

Samuel made a note in his notebook, then looked up with a questioning expression. "Why don't you seem more enthusiastic about communicating with your relatives?"

Grace took a deep breath, trying to steady her emotions. "It's not that they're bad people. They are kind and well-meaning. But the day after I arrived, we were back at long, monotonous family gatherings. I appreciated their stories and memories—they tried to fill the gap left by my parents. But it felt like too much. I thought I needed more attention and affection, but maybe I was wrong."

Samuel's brow furrowed slightly. "Explain."

Grace's voice trembled as she spoke. "When William and Monica left me in the background, I craved attention and parental love. But with the Freemans, it felt overwhelming. Inside, I felt like I was betraying my parents. I felt guilty for accepting their affection when I knew it wasn't the same. Later, I found out they couldn't have children of their own and saw an opportunity to find parental happiness with me. But I'm not their child, and they're not my parents. After a week, I moved into a hostel near the college to get some personal space."

Samuel's gaze pierced through the room, his lips curling into a faint smile. "So, do you want parents or not?"

Grace hesitated, a look of confusion crossing her face. "I don't know... I thought I did, but it's complicated."

Samuel's smile widened, though it remained enigmatic. "Hmm, we'll explore that together. For now, tell me about the university. How did you feel? What do you remember?"

—◊◊—

The days at the university stretched into what felt like months. Early mornings, back-to-back classes, quick lunches, more classes, dinner, homework, and finally, sleep. Grace's life had settled into a monotonous routine of endless gray days. Learning came easily to her—studying became a refuge from her obsessive thoughts. By immersing herself in every detail of her subjects, Grace earned the respect of her professors, who held a favorable view of her diligent work ethic.

Despite her academic success, Grace never formed real friendships. Her inconsistency made it difficult to forge lasting connections. She had enough energy only for brief acquaintances and superficial conversations, which she quickly grew tired of. She preferred to spend most of her time in isolation, longing to remain locked away in her room, avoiding the world outside. Each morning, her mood sank to zero, and she wished only to collapse into bed and stay there. She spent most weekends in this despondent state. Her emotions were elusive, changing inexplicably, leaving her enveloped in a pervasive sadness that seemed inescapable.

In her small, self-imposed world, Grace found a semblance of comfort. One day, driven by a need to unload her accumulated feelings, she made an entry in her old diary. She hoped to express what she couldn't voice aloud. Her writing revealed her inner turmoil:

"The alarm...

Once again, my heart pounds in a frenzied rhythm. It feels tight in my chest. Awareness comes slowly and painfully. I feel like I can't stand it. This endless monotony—university and homework, classmates and the Freemans—it's so stifling. Words fail me... I just feel bad. As usual. I want to cry. As usual. I long to write something deep and beautiful. It doesn't come. My heart feels heavy. As usual. Where do I find strength?

Where is my inner core?! Am I really that weak? I've been told to be strong and smart since childhood. Maybe I should write something more positive. It might make me seem like I'm just complaining. I want to feel lightness and joy, happiness and love. I'm tired of my own complaints, of feeling like no one cares. And, as always, I'll begin to torment myself with doubts and despair... I hope that someday I'll read these pages, laugh at this naïve girl, and say, she made it through."

—m—

The diary entry offered brief solace, but soon her despondency returned, painting her world in deeper shades of gray. Missing a few lectures and failing an intermediate test left Grace feeling hollow. Guilt and shame eluded her. Returning home, she noticed a poster advertising a party at one of the fraternities. Normally, Grace had no interest in alcohol, dancing, or meeting new people. But that day, she yearned for something different, a break from the relentless monotony and her incessant worries.

—m—

"Are you serious?!"

"HAHAHAHA!"

"Therefore, democracy is complete..."

"Come on!!!"

"No one loves me..."

"Drown him!!!"

"Grace?!"

"Careful!"

66

"It's getting started in here!!!"

"Hold her hair!"

"Hello,"

All the voices merged into one. Grace perceived the world in all its essence. A conversation with one person, incomprehensibly, turned into dancing with another. A few moments ago, the girl completely forgot about everything that was happening. The music was felt, not heard. The body moved spontaneously, without any commands from the wearer.

"Do you want to dilute the fun?" a girl she didn't know offered Grace, her voice dripping with an unsettling allure.

"What are you talking about?" Grace giggled with an edge of manic curiosity.

The girl pulled out a bag of pills from her pocket and pointed toward the sofa with a seductive smirk.

"Uh…" Grace hesitated, the edges of her perception blurring.

"Come on!" The stranger's hand was insistent as she guided Grace to the sofa.

They sank down together. The stranger bit off a piece of the pill and offered the remaining part to Grace. Hesitantly, Grace brought it to her mouth, her hands trembling slightly. The stranger's eyes gleamed with an unnerving approval. She then produced a glass device that looked like a vase with a narrow bottom, its surface gleaming ominously.

"What is it?" Grace asked, her voice wobbling as she took the pill.

"Inhale," the stranger instructed, her tone almost hypnotic.

Grace took a deep breath, drawing the substance into her lungs. A harsh cough erupted uncontrollably.

"Oh, I envy you so much," the girl said, her laughter echoing eerily. "How are you? Do you feel anything?"

Grace's coughing subsided, and she choked out, "Yes, no. It's just hard in my lungs, but…" Her voice trailed off as the warmth began to spread through her body.

Her pupils dilated, absorbing the encroaching sensations. A deep, enveloping warmth flooded her senses, like pleasant goosebumps that spread over her skin. Grace slumped onto the couch, her body relaxing, the feeling both soothing and disorienting.

"Sort of… I feel…" she mumbled, her fingers tracing the sofa's surface as if it was an entirely unfamiliar sensation. "Is this the world spinning… or me? Haha, I'm closing my eyes… and the smile appears on its own. I wish I could go to the beach now…"

Suddenly, a wave of warmth enveloped her entire body, akin to sunbathing under intense, radiant beams. As Grace sunk into the couch, the pulse of the music seemed to sync with her heartbeat, each beat resonating deeply within her. The surrounding room shimmered, the colors blending into a surreal, ethereal tapestry. What had been a mundane party now felt like a vibrant dreamscape, where every sound, sight, and touch was amplified by an extraordinary sensory experience.

Her body felt light, almost as though she were floating. The sensation of the sofa beneath her was transformed into something velvety and warm, like lying on a cloud. Each breath she took was smooth and deep, filling her lungs with a soothing warmth that spread through her entire being.

The music, once just a backdrop, was now a living, breathing entity. The melodies flowed through her, wrapping around her senses like a comforting embrace. Each note seemed to dance and pulsate with a rhythm that resonated with her very core. She felt as if she were moving with the music, her body swaying and undulating in perfect harmony with the beats.

A cascade of feelings—an effervescent joy that bubbled up from within. As the pill took effect, her pupils dilated, and the world around her became more vivid, more profound.

The sofa felt like an extension of her body, its texture more refined and its comfort more exquisite. Grace's hand traced the contours of the couch, the sensation of the fabric against her skin sending ripples of pleasure through her. Every touch felt like a revelation, a new sensation of warmth and softness that she never wanted to end.

As the heavenly sensations continued to alter her perception, Grace found herself laughing with abandon, the joy spilling out of her effortlessly. The dance floor became a sea of moving lights and shifting shapes, each person a radiant beacon of energy and connection. She felt a deep, unspoken bond with those around her, as if she could see their inner light shining through.

"Haha… Sarah would love this…" Grace smiled softly, her thoughts drifting. "She loved Hawaii. But we had a fight…" Her voice quivered with sadness.

"You can still make up!" a new voice interrupted, smooth and unsettling.

"Sarah?!" Grace exclaimed, turning toward the voice.

"Nah, not even close." The figure crouched down, its face now a distorted mask of familiarity. The figure's eyes glowed with a disturbing intensity as it looked into Grace's face.

"Andrew! What are you doing here?"

"Having fun, just like everyone else," the hallucination of her former classmate replied, sitting with an unnerving calm. He gestured toward the swirling crowd, where shadows danced and writhed. "How's Sarah?"

"Yes, she often talks about you. Why don't you ask her yourself?" Andrew suggested, pointing to the retreating girl in the dress.

"Sarah! Wait!" Grace's voice was a desperate cry as she tried to follow.

She fled from the building, her heart pounding as she chased after Sarah. The blonde crown kept slipping from her view, and a flower of anticipation bloomed within her, driving her frantic rush.

"Sarah!" Grace called out, her voice cracking with urgency.

Turning the corner, she continued running, her breath coming in ragged gasps. "Agh, wait a minute!" she shouted, stopping to catch her breath.

When Grace saw Sarah talking to two people, her heart froze in her chest. Their faces were horribly familiar. Blinking rapidly, she struggled to believe her eyes.

"Mom?! Dad?!" Grace's voice cracked with a mix of joy and dread.

Lillian and Richard turned slowly, their expressions twisted with anger and a cold, haunting disapproval. Their eyes seemed to bore into Grace, making her heart ache with an unbearable pain. Tears welled up in her eyes.

"What's wrong?" Grace whispered, her voice barely a breath. "What did I do?" she asked, glancing around in disarray. A wooden bedside table from her old house loomed behind her, an ominous reminder of home.

"Grace!" The voice of her mother came down the stairs, but it was eerie and distorted. Lillian, in her favorite floral dress, appeared almost ghostly, her warmth now a chilling memory.

"Mom!" Grace cried out, reaching for her mother's embrace. "I missed you so much!" she said, tears streaming down her face. "Where's Dad?" she asked, her voice trembling with fear.

"He's starting the car. We're going to Sarah's birthday party," her mother said, her voice hollow and echoing unnervingly.

A cold sweat broke out on Grace's forehead. She broke free from her mother's embrace, running to the door with mounting terror. She screamed at the top of her lungs.

The girl opened the door, only to find herself back in her house, as if the outside world had never existed. Confused, she saw Richard sitting at the table, eating his favorite soup with an unsettling calmness.

"I definitely left the house. Why is everything so wrong?" Grace wondered, her mind racing. She didn't have time to ponder the oddities. Something more pressing weighed on her.

"The car! The tire is flat!" she shouted, rushing to her father.

"What do you mean?" Richard asked, his tone disturbingly nonchalant. "I just arrived on it," he said, tearing off a slice of bread.

Grace rushed outside to check the car. The wheel was perfectly intact. "But it was damaged! What's happening?" she thought, bewildered, as she returned inside. The atmosphere grew heavy, and the sensation of impending doom intensified.

"Hahaha," a child's laughter echoed behind her, a sinister note in the sound.

Grace turned around, her heart pounding, and saw a horrifying vision. A little girl with monstrous yellow eyes, styled blond curls, and a twisted, mocking smile danced away from the car, her face a grotesque version of Grace's own as a child.

"What?" Grace whispered in disbelief. She dashed to the car and saw the flat tire, her memories of the day now a distorted blur.

"I flattened the tire…" Grace's thoughts were a chaotic whirl, trying to piece together the fractured memories.

"Daughter! Why did you run out?" came the distorted voices of her parents.

Grace stood frozen by the flat tire, paralyzed with fear.

"Is everything okay?" Richard and Lillian rushed to her side, their faces etched with a disturbing blend of concern and menace.

Grace pointed to the flat tire with a trembling hand. Richard examined it with a grim expression.

"Why did you do that?" Lillian asked, her hands cold and vice-like on Grace's shoulders. Her smile was a grotesque, frozen mask.

"It's not me!" Grace cried out.

"It's okay, everything is fixable," Richard said, his gaze growing more intense. "Except for this…" he began, but his words were cut off…

Grace's horror peaked as she met Richard's gaze. His face and body were grotesquely disfigured from the accident, his head hanging at an unnatural angle.

"Oh no, oh no, oh no!" Grace backed away, her screams piercing the air.

Her mother's warm embrace turned cold and suffocating. Her touch was harsh, her expression unmoving and ominous.

"My Lady, don't be so scared. Who hasn't faced such things?" the stranger's voice came from Lillian's place. He appeared, a shadowy figure with an aura of menace. He tossed stones up and down, his movements unnervingly fluid. Her parents stood behind him, manipulated like marionettes by invisible strings.

"AAAAAAA!" Grace screamed in terror, her voice echoing in the nightmarish vision.

"Grace!" her parents rushed into the room, their concern genuine but tinged with an unsettling edge.

"What happened?" her mother asked anxiously, a beacon of comfort amidst the chaos.

"Nightmare…" Grace said, "I dreamed you died in an accident." She clung to Lillian, her fear overwhelming.

"My girl!" her mother's voice was soothing, but it carried an unsettling edge. "You can go to bed, dear. I'll stay with you for now." She touched her husband's shoulder gently.

After a tender kiss on Grace's forehead, Richard left the room.

Lillian lay down beside Grace, her familiar lullabies now strangely eerie. Her favorite teddy bear sat on the bedside table, holding a basket of flowers with an unnatural stillness. In her mother's embrace, Grace felt a strange mixture of comfort and dread as she closed her eyes again, slipping back into a dream that seemed more real than reality.

A moment passed. Grace's eyes opened, and it was as if nothing had happened before, but the fear lingered.

A kiss at the prom. Happy parents. Life seemed like a fairy tale. Grace closed the door behind Andrew, her heart brimming with joy. As she gazed at her reflection in the mirror, a satisfied smile graced her lips. She imagined a future bathed in light: a big white house, a sprawling garden—everything perfect and pristine.

"You look incredible!" Sarah exclaimed, holding a glass of sparkling champagne, her eyes shining with excitement.

"Thank you," Grace replied, her voice soft as she adjusted her hairstyle.

"It's starting!" Sarah said with a grin, her enthusiasm barely contained. She squeezed Grace's shoulder tightly and hurried off to the ceremony.

"Come here!" Richard's arms were open wide, his face alight with pride and love.

"Dad!" Grace felt a wave of nostalgia wash over her as she embraced him. "I love you and I'm so proud of you!" Richard's voice was tender, his eyes glistening with emotion. "Let's go, it's starting!"

The wedding music played, and the faces around her were illuminated with joy as her father escorted Grace to the pedestal. Richard led her to Andrew, who stood waiting with a look of adoration. Richard smiled at his daughter before taking his place next to Lillian.

Andrew's gaze was filled with love as he saw Grace for the first time that day. She reached out her arms to him, her heart overflowing with happiness.

"Do you swear, Grace Bailey, to love Andrew Brown for better or worse?" the pastor intoned.

"Yes!" Grace's voice trembled with tears of joy.

"And do you, Andrew Brown, swear to love Grace Bailey for better or worse?"

"Yes!" Andrew's voice was steady, his eyes locked on Grace's.

"Are you ready to move into a new stage of your life?" the pastor asked, his tone now tinged with an unsettling undertone.

"Yes!" Grace replied eagerly.

"Are you ready to live your remaining days on this earth with the sin of regrets?" the pastor's voice turned ominous, sending shivers down Grace's spine.

"What?" Grace's confusion deepened as she glanced at the pastor.

"Are you ready to wake up every day and fall asleep every night with a heavy sense of guilt?" the pastor's tone was chilling, his eyes piercing.

"I don't understand," Grace stammered, her gaze shifting to Andrew's suddenly cold expression.

"My lady, you should have shown your parents the flat tire," the stranger, now revealed in the pastor's guise, explained with a deranged gleam in his eyes.

The red eyes bore into Grace's soul. The stranger's lips stretched into a grotesque, maniacal grin as he burst into loud, frenzied laughter. Grace's heart pounded as she released Andrew's cold, unfeeling hands. He pushed her away with a look of disgust. Terrified, Grace stumbled back, barely avoiding a collision with Sarah.

Sarah's face twisted with rage as she hurled a small bouquet at Grace, thorns digging into her skin. Dark, thick blood oozed from the wounds, mingling with Grace's tears.

"Don't come into my life anymore," Sarah spat out before taking Andrew's hand. They walked away, their figures slowly disappearing into a thick, suffocating fog. Grace watched in shock, her mind reeling from the nightmarish scene.

A chilling voice came from behind her.

"What do you think? Will your parents forgive you?" The stranger's sinister smile widened.

Turning slowly, Grace's gaze fell upon the disfigured corpses of her parents. Richard and Lillian lay in a state of grotesque decay, their bodies emitting a foul stench of rot and a sickly sweet odor of death. Their lifeless eyes stared at Grace with an accusatory glare. A tear trickled down Lillian's decayed cheek. Richard's eyes burned with an intense, unrelenting fury.

"Oh my God," Grace whispered in horror, her heart racing uncontrollably. The image burned itself into her mind, an indelible scar of terror.

"No, no, no, My Lady. There is no God here," the stranger whispered menacingly into Grace's ear. His devilish laughter reverberated through the church, echoing off the walls with a chilling finality.

"I was invited to a party," Grace said, her voice barely more than a whisper. "I went too far and woke up on the floor the next morning. The dorm supervisor found me and reported it to the university. That's how I ended up here," she explained, her eyes fixed on the floor.

Sam scribbled in his notebook, his gaze briefly lifting to meet hers. "What was the party like?"

"Just... a party," Grace replied, her tone distant. "Dancing, music, booze," she added, her words clipped as if she were reciting a well-worn script.

"Why did you go?" Sam asked, his curiosity tinged with concern. "You don't seem like someone who enjoys that kind of scene."

Grace's eyes drifted to the vase on the table, its delicate porcelain stark against the stark white of the room. She shivered slightly, not from the cold but from a deeper, unsettling chill. "After the fight with Sarah, everything felt pointless," she admitted, her voice heavy with fatigue. "The days ran together, and talking to students felt like a contest of who could pretend the hardest. I was just so tired—tired of the dark thoughts, the pointless lectures, and the Freemans. They're good people, but I don't fit in. I needed a break from it all."

Sam's pen paused mid-sentence as he absorbed her words. He glanced at his watch and then back at Grace, his expression unreadable. "Well, Miss Bailey," he said, his voice a mix of detached professionalism and reluctant sympathy, "this could be seen as progress. Unfortunately, our time is almost up. Try not to drown in your thoughts. It's pointless to blame yourself, even if you feel guilty. As for Sarah, perhaps you should reach out to her before our next session and let me know how it goes."

Grace's gaze was distant, her thoughts swirling like a storm. "Okay, doctor. Thank you," she murmured, the words feeling hollow and inadequate.

"See you soon," Sam said, his smile thin and unconvincing as he returned to his notes.

As Grace stepped out of the office, the flowered wallpaper seemed to shift and pulse, reflecting the chaos inside her mind. The small spark of hope she had clung to was fading fast, lost in the growing darkness that she could neither escape nor fully confront. The room seemed to close in on her, a silent witness to her unraveling.

"Yeah…" Grace whispered hollowly, exiting the room.

Grace trudged along the wet, winding road, raindrops battering her face with relentless force. The storm mirrored the tempest inside her, a cacophony of shadows from her past. "Of course," she thought, her mind weighed down by sorrow. "Life has turned out to be so difficult. The memories are heavy, and my thoughts are suffocating. Tomorrow is supposed to be a new beginning—a new day, new people, new moments. Adult life is ready to take over from the turbulence of adolescence. But I'm still old Grace, carrying scars and wounds that cannot be simply erased. To start over would mean forgetting Sarah, her love for caramel ice cream, her funny habit of frowning in photos, and the way she'd offer the last piece of chocolate despite wanting it for herself. Her smile meant more to Sarah than her own satisfaction."

The image of Sarah's face, filled with shock, resentment, and anger, clawed at Grace's heart, leaving an indelible mark of pain. The memory was a dark stain on her soul, a haunting presence she could never escape.

Sarah's parents, though not her real parents, had shown Grace kindness in their own way. Their warm smiles and rare hugs had been a source of comfort. Sometimes, Grace felt their pride and love, albeit different from what one might expect from biological parents. Would they ever fully accept her, love her like their own, and forget that she wasn't truly their daughter? It felt too late for that. The cozy fragrance of their home was a distant memory she could never return to.

Andrew was another painful memory, bright and cheerful, like a beacon of warmth that she could never quite grasp. With him, she felt truly valued. Yet, his heart, his hands, and his tender gaze were never meant for her. The summer nights they spent together, laughing and listening to their favorite songs, seemed like a cruel mirage now. The depth of his eyes had once been a comforting warmth, akin to a cup of hot chocolate in the cold, but now, without that comfort, she felt like she was freezing to death.

Her father's image was a bittersweet echo of the past. "Oh, Grace, you look just like your father," her aunt would say with a smile. "Yes," little Grace would reply proudly, believing her dad was the most handsome man in the world. "I'm strong, Grace," he'd reassure her, holding her close after a rough day. "If anyone hurts you, just tell me." In those moments, with her father by her side, the world seemed less frightening. "Papa, you're home!" she would shout with glee when he returned, always bringing sweets, despite her mother's disapproval. It was a tradition he maintained until the end.

The wind ruffled Grace's hair, her legs covered in goosebumps as the sky darkened into deep shades. It was as if an artist was painting a somber masterpiece, using a palette of gray with hints of bitterness and salty tears.

"It's so cold," Grace murmured, trying to recall her mother's face. Her gentle hands braiding Grace's hair, always adorned with bows she loved. Lillian's words echoed in her memory: "This is a pink tulip—the flower of love and happiness. My sweet Grace, you are my tulip." Her mother had always been a sunny presence, her emotions sometimes tinged with sadness, but never fully captured in Grace's fading recollections. Her eyes had been a blur—brown, or greenish? Her voice, though clear and melodic, was slipping away.

Grace sank slowly to her knees, her movements graceful, as if yielding to a gentle breeze. She placed a hand over her heart, feeling its fragile beat, and gazed up at the stormy sky. The rain intensified, mingling with her tears.

Her heartbeat, once a steady rhythm, began to pound violently against her chest, each beat resonating like a distant drum of doom. It seemed to grow louder, echoing through the darkness, a desperate, frantic percussion of her inner turmoil. The pounding was relentless, a constant reminder of her anguish.

Suddenly, an ear-splitting scream erupted from Grace's throat. It was a bone-chilling, primal sound—a cry that seemed to tear through the very fabric of the night. The scream was raw, a manifestation of her profound despair and hopelessness. It reverberated through the storm, mingling with the howling wind and crashing rain, a haunting melody of grief and torment.

Grace's scream pierced the storm, a desperate wail that seemed to make the heavens shudder. It was a sound that spoke of a heart breaking under the weight of its own sorrow, a sound that would linger in the air long after the storm had passed. As her cry faded into the distance, the rain continued to pour, relentless and unforgiving, as if nature itself was mourning with her.

—⟋⟍—

The sky had cleared after the storm, but the sun was nowhere to be seen. Instead, a deep, all-consuming darkness blanketed the heavens, rendering the celestial space an unending void.

Grace returned to her small room, the noise of the bustling building eerily absent. It was "Thanksgiving Day," a family holiday, and she was alone—an ironic twist, given the celebration of togetherness.

The door to her room creaked open, revealing a dimly lit interior. As Grace flicked on the light switch, a harsh, cold illumination flooded the space, casting stark shadows on the walls.

The room was a dismal gray, marred by cracks and a pervasive sense of neglect. The bed, with its thin white railing, was crammed into a corner. Textbooks, notebooks, and various discarded items cluttered the table—an old tube of lip gloss, an empty beer can with a gum wrapper stuffed inside, and crumpled paper strewn around the trash can. It was as if someone who no longer cared about order or cleanliness had abandoned the room.

A faint, unpleasant odor of rotting food lingered in the air, adding to the sense of decay. A crumpled bag from a fast-food joint lay discarded by the bed.

The sparse light barely penetrated the gloom of the room. Only near the window could one catch a glimpse of the sunlit cityscape and a small playground below.

Grace's tear-stained eyes scanned the familiar, dreary surroundings. The darkness outside seemed to mirror the darkness within her soul. She moved slowly towards the window, the floorboards creaking ominously under her weight. Her gaze fixated on the asphalt below, her lips barely twitching in a semblance of a smile.

"Nine floors," she murmured, her thoughts detached and mechanical.

She opened the window, feeling the icy wind brush against her face. Her eyelids fluttered closed as her senses sharpened—the distant song of birds, the honking of cars, the murmur of the wind caressing the buildings, children's laughter and cries. Standing at the very edge of the window, Grace's fear of heights seemed to dissolve. It was as if she were preparing to step through the air, ready to leave the world behind.

"Nine floors... 30 meters... three seconds..."

The fear of heights vanished, replaced by a surreal sensation that she might walk through the air. Her heart beat with a deafening, chaotic rhythm.

"Knock... knock... knock..."

The sounds pierced through her, painfully familiar. Grace recoiled from the window, her pulse racing with dread. The sensation of déjà vu overwhelmed her.

"Is that really it?... no! Not happening... Or maybe?"

A shuddering fear engulfed her as she stared at the door. She took tentative steps toward it, her body trembling. The lock on the door provided a false sense of security. Adrenaline coursed through her veins. Peering through the peephole, she saw a familiar face.

"Doctor?!" Grace's voice trembled with a mix of relief and confusion.

The door creaked open, and Sam stepped into the room.

Grace's mind reeled. "I closed the door... How...?"

"Don't worry, it happens sometimes, but all doors are open for me," Sam said with a sinister smile, showing the keyhole. "What's the matter, my Lady? You look scared."

"My Lady?" Grace's eyes widened with terror at the word.

Sam snapped his fingers. Instantly, the door swung open, revealing the empty hostel lobby.

"Now I'll explain what's going to happen," Sam said, his tone turning grave. "All your fears, resentments, feelings of guilt will project into reality. Your task is to let them go in your mind; otherwise, they will manifest here."

Before he could continue, a familiar, deranged laugh echoed through the hall. A disheveled figure appeared, clutching stones in his hands.

"Well, hello! How are you? And you've grown up!" the stranger said with a twisted grin.

Grace screamed, stumbling backward. Her heart pounded in a frenzy.

"No, no, no, come on! Quite the opposite!" Sam said, still sitting in the chair with an eerie calmness. Grace's back collided with something solid—her father's grotesque, decomposing corpse.

"Dad?!" Her voice broke into a desperate sob. The sight of her father's lifeless body overwhelmed her, her reality crumbling. She fell to the floor, curled into a ball, trying to block out the horror.

"I repeat once again," Sam's voice cut through the chaos with chilling clarity, "only you can prevent what is happening. Let go of your sins, stop blaming yourself, and everything will pass."

Grace screamed, her voice raw and broken. "Stop it! Please! Let them disappear!"

Sam's smile was predatory. "Sin number one! Pride! You ignored a flat tire and killed your parents!"

"No! No! It wasn't like that!" Grace clawed at the floor, tears streaming.

"Sin number two! Envy of your best friend, leading to the end of your friendship and your love."

"I didn't mean to!" Grace's pleas were desperate, her voice choked.

"Everything can still be changed," Sam's voice took on a false note of hope as Andrew's figure appeared. Grace's heart leapt, but her hope quickly turned to dread as she saw the horrifying scene unfold before her.

"Sin number three..." Sam's tone grew softer, but his gaze was piercing. "You know it yourself."

"That's enough! Please! Stop it!!!" Grace begged, her voice breaking into incoherence.

Sam clapped his hands twice. The room fell into a suffocating silence. Grace stood, trembling and gasping for air.

"Your choice?" Sam's voice was cold and calculating. "Have you ever wondered what your life might have been like if you hadn't succumbed to the demons of your past?"

Grace stared blankly at the dismembered figure of her dead father, her eyes red and swollen. "My choice..."

Without a word, Grace ran to the window, her heart pounding as she looked down at the abyss below. She took a deep breath, closed her eyes, and jumped.

The weight of Sam's words crushed her. Her gaze was vacant, her spirit shattered. With a final, resolute motion, without a word, Grace ran to the window, her heart pounding as she looked down at the abyss below. She took a deep breath, closed her eyes and leaped into the void.

The emptiness enveloped her as she plummeted, her scream echoing through the abyss. It was a cry of finality, a release from the torment that had consumed her.

The city below grew closer, and the darkness swallowed her whole.

In the aftermath, Sam stood alone in Grace's room, his expression inscrutable. He walked over to the window to observe the lifeless body sprawled on the asphalt and glanced at the empty, darkened sky outside. With deliberate movements, he pulled out his notebook—a worn, black book filled with the detailed accounts of his sessions. He flipped through the pages until he found Grace's name. With a slow, deliberate stroke, he crossed out "Grace Bailey."

"Goodbye, Grace," he said softly, a cruel edge to his voice. His gaze shifted to the demons lurking in the shadows of the room.

"Leave this realm," The Devil commanded, his voice a dark, imperious decree. The demons, trembling before the king of Hell, obeyed without question. With a final, menacing look at the room, he noticed dead flowers among the trash and let out an eerie smile. Samuel turned and walked out, leaving behind a realm of despair.

WITHERED ROSE

Kemal Tabyldy

CHAPTER

1

The dimly lit hall echoed with the muffled sounds of footsteps, a chilling reminder of the souls that roamed its depths. A middle-aged man emerged from the shadows, moving with a smooth yet confident gait. His highly polished business shoes, gray sweater, and trousers gave him a classically simple appearance. But his proudly raised head, precise steps, and free movements exuded a sense of ownership over this infernal realm.

As he moved through the corridor, the dead silence was interrupted by sounds seeping through the doors lining the hall. At first glance, it seemed as though he was walking a straight path. However, the corridor flowed in serpentine curves, like the winding coils of a snake. The doors stood at different levels, each one exuding a different aura of torment. Bitter guttural crying came from one, manic laughter from another, and quiet screams from a third. The further he walked, the more varied and intense the sounds became, yet he continued with unwavering confidence.

Finally, he stopped at a particular door and checked his watch. The time showed 5:59. Patiently waiting for the last minute, surrounded by muffled voices and the heavy, oppressive air, he watched as the clock moved forward. At precisely 6:00, he knocked on the door.

"Come in..." a hoarse, broken voice responded from the other side.

Entering the room, the man was met by an elderly, unkempt figure. It was difficult to determine his age; he could have been 60, 90, or thousands of years old. His clothes were torn and filthy, his hands wrapped in old, dirty bandages, and his feet covered by worn-out, leaky shoes. He reeked of alcohol and stale sweat, his skin pocked and yellowed from years of substance abuse.

The man briefly assessed the room. Empty glass bottles and used syringes littered the floor, and the air was thick with the stench of decay. A dim lamp on the ceiling cast a sickly yellow light, attracting aimlessly-flying moths. A worktable stood to one side, covered in crumpled paper and a vase of wilted flowers. In the center of the room sat the old man, glued to a wooden chair, his eyes bloodshot and filled with a mix of hatred and despair.

"How are you?" the man asked coldly, his voice carrying an unsettling authority.

"Can't you see?" the old man responded blankly, his voice a gravelly rasp. "Miserable..."

Grinning with a hint of malice, the man turned his attention to the table. "Why don't you change the flowers?"

"What's the point of changing them? They'll wither in a day or two anyway," the old man snapped, his voice filled with bitterness. "Speaking of days, how long have I been here? I don't remember the first day in this damn room. I've lost track of time long ago..."

"What's the point of knowing? Knowing won't change anything anyway," the man repeated, his tone dripping with irony.

The old man looked down, his expression a mix of anger and resignation.

"Perhaps you would like to know... how to change your life?" the man suggested aloofly, his eyes glinting with a sinister promise as he circled the room.

The old man's once dull eyes filled with a flicker of hope and childish delight. "Yes! Please! Tell me how!" he pleaded in a hoarse voice, throwing himself at the feet of the newcomer, his desperation palpable.

"I doubt you will be able to do it. You'll probably give up not even on the tenth, but on the second attempt," the man explained coldly, his words cutting deep.

"I'll do anything! I swear!" the old man begged, his voice trembling with desperation.

The man looked disinterestedly towards the exit and walked to the door.

"I can do it! Give me a chance! I beg you!" the old man cried out, his voice cracking.

The man looked down at the old man and said, "Okay, listen carefully," his tone serious and commanding.

The old man nodded vigorously, staring at him expectantly on his knees, his eyes wide with hope.

"First, clean up the room and change the flowers in the vase," the man instructed, his voice echoing with a chilling finality.

In a shadowy corner of the room, the dim light barely revealed the figure of a young boy, his blue eyes wide with concern as they darted towards the woman lying motionless on the floor.

"Mom? Is everything okay?" Andrew's voice quivered as he peeked around the corner. His blue eyes widened in fear at the sight of the woman lying motionless on the floor.

"Andrew! Come here!" his father barked, anger crackling in his voice. Seated in a chair, the man's fingers gripped a cigarette, its orange glow casting menacing shadows. He jabbed his finger toward the floor, his gaze sharp and unyielding.

Andrew hesitated, his small body trembling with fear. At just five years old, he was well-acquainted with the stench of cigarette smoke and alcohol that clung to his father. The looming dread of his father's fury made his stomach churn, and he could barely keep his legs steady. The sight of his father's cruel, unblinking eyes paralyzed him with terror.

"Is Mom okay?" Andrew managed to ask, his voice barely more than a whisper, quaking under the weight of his father's gaze.

"She upset me," his father said with a cold sneer, using the cigarette to point disdainfully at the woman's lifeless form. "You don't want to upset me, do you?"

"No..." Andrew's voice was a frightened whisper, his head shaking involuntarily. He was fighting back tears, every fiber of his being consumed by fear of the inevitable.

Without warning, his father's hand grabbed Andrew's left hand with a rough, unfeeling grip. A cruel smile spread across his face as he pressed the burning cigarette against the boy's tender skin. The searing pain was instantaneous and excruciating, as if his hand were being engulfed in molten fire. Andrew's scream erupted from deep within him, a high-pitched wail of agony that seemed to tear through his entire being.

"AAH!!! Ahh!!! Daddy! It hurts! Stop it!" Andrew cried out, his voice breaking into frantic sobs. The pain was relentless, a blinding, all-consuming torment that made his entire body writhe and convulse.

"Yes... don't twitch," his father muttered coldly. "It'll only hurt more." He pressed the cigarette harder into Andrew's flesh, savoring the boy's suffering.

"It hurts! Ah! Ah! AAH!! Daddy, please!!!!" Andrew screamed, his voice raw with pain as he watched the smoke rising from his hand. Each moment felt like an eternity of suffering, and he could barely breathe through the agony.

"Stop it!" the drunk man roared, his anger erupting. "You're a man! Act like it!" he shouted, his hand connecting with Andrew's chest in a forceful, violent blow.

The impact knocked Andrew to the floor, gasping for breath as pain radiated from his chest. He scrambled to his mother, his cries a desperate plea for comfort amidst the chaos.

"Mom! Mommy! Wake up!" Andrew shouted, shaking her lifeless body with frantic desperation.

The father, now standing, grabbed a bottle and began to drink greedily, as if it were a lifeline.

"Shit!" he roared in frustration, hurling the bottle aside. It shattered, the sound of breaking glass adding to the oppressive atmosphere.

Andrew, trembling in fear, cowered behind his mother. He covered his head with his hands, bracing against the noise of the broken bottle and his father's enraged shouts.

"Where did this bitch hide my money?!" the man screamed, tearing through the room and flinging open shelves with reckless anger. "Ema!" he shouted, glaring at the woman with a contemptuous look.

The child, shivering with terror, crawled as far away from his father as he could. The man, fuming with rage, stormed out of the house, leaving Andrew and his mother in the oppressive darkness.

When the door slammed shut, the boy slowly lowered his arms, his fear mingled with the heavy silence. He blinked, adjusting to the dim shapes of the room, and carefully crawled on all fours towards his mother's body.

"Mom?" he called out softly, his voice trembling with uncertainty. He gently tugged at her hair, trying to rouse her, confusion and dread clouding his young mind.

Wrapping himself in his mother's lifeless embrace, Andrew lay next to her, seeking solace in the cold comfort of her still form. In the darkness, the sharp edges of his pain seemed to dull, and the once-soothing sensation of her arms around him now felt like a fragile illusion of safety.

"ANDREW!!!" a hoarse, guttural scream pierced the silence, calling for the boy.

—⁂—

Abruptly, Andrew's eyes shot open, his heart racing and breath coming in labored gasps. The dingy room seemed to close in on him as he desperately tried to orient himself. His gaze fell on Sarah, her presence a comforting anchor in the storm of his thoughts. He took a deep breath, eyes closed tightly, and rubbed his temples in a vain attempt to ward off the lingering sense of dread.

Sarah's eyes, filled with concern, never left him. "How are you?" she asked softly, her voice a gentle balm against the harshness of his thoughts.

"Fine," Andrew replied curtly, his tone betraying his desire to keep the true extent of his turmoil buried deep within. He offered a weak smile, but it didn't quite reach his eyes.

His attention drifted to the scar on his body, a grotesque reminder of past suffering. The burn, a ragged line of discolored skin, pulsed faintly with discomfort. Andrew's fingers brushed over the mark, a futile attempt to ease the ache that seemed to flare up whenever his mind wandered to darker places.

The relentless beeping of the alarm clock shattered the silence, its sound jarring and intrusive. The clock, old and worn, seemed to be a cruel reminder of the grinding monotony of their lives. Andrew reached out, fingers trembling slightly as he turned off the alarm, the metal cold against his skin.

Sarah, her face etched with worry, placed a reassuring hand on Andrew's shoulder. Her touch was warm and comforting, a stark contrast to the coldness that often pervaded their lives. Andrew kissed her hand gently, a tender gesture that masked the turmoil bubbling beneath the surface. He wanted to share his burdens with her but hesitated, unwilling to add to her own struggles.

The door swung open with a creak, and Noah and baby Rene rushed into the room. The faded wallpaper and threadbare carpet of their modest home bore witness to the poverty that clung to them. Noah, with his unrestrained energy, leaped onto the bed, landing heavily on Andrew's stomach and driving the breath from his lungs.

"Daddy! Mommy! Good morning!" they exclaimed, their voices high with excitement.

"Careful, guys," Andrew chuckled, despite the pain. He laughed heartily, a sound that masked the exhaustion he felt. The weight of his son was a temporary distraction from the grinding reality of their lives.

Sarah joined in the laughter, her voice a bright contrast to the squalor that surrounded them. "You little monkeys, come here!" she said, her eyes crinkling with affection as she gathered the children into a loving embrace.

The bed was a tattered haven, the blanket thin but comforting. Noah curled up against Andrew, falling asleep almost instantly, while Rene sprawled out with a carefree abandon, her tiny legs stretching across the worn sheets.

Andrew carefully held Rene's small, cold foot, his fingers brushing over Noah's tousled hair with a tenderness that spoke of deep love and hidden pain. He met Sarah's gaze, and their silent exchange was filled with mutual understanding and unspoken fears.

The alarm clock blared again, its insistent noise cutting through the fragile peace of their morning. "Well, shall we?" Andrew asked, trying to muster a cheerfulness he didn't quite feel.

"Yeah," Sarah replied, stretching languidly and brushing a strand of hair from her face. She moved with a graceful ease, her actions betraying none of the fatigue she felt.

Andrew headed to the shower, seeking solace in its warm embrace. The shower stall, a cramped space with peeling tiles and a broken handle, was a stark contrast to the promise of comfort it offered. The warm water cascaded over him, but even this small luxury was tinged with the harsh realities of their situation.

A sudden jolt of cold water made Andrew flinch, his irritation rising. "The water's cold!" he shouted, his frustration palpable. The shoddy plumbing and irregular water supply were constant reminders of their financial struggles.

After a few moments of exasperation, Andrew wrapped himself in a threadbare towel and stepped out of the shower, his irritation simmering beneath the surface. He returned to his morning routine, trying to push aside the remnants of his restless night and the oppressive weight of their poverty. Despite his attempts to keep his struggles hidden, Sarah's concerned eyes followed him, her silent support a steadying presence in their tumultuous lives.

—∿—

"Smells delicious!" Andrew called from the bedroom, his voice carrying a mix of excitement and gratitude.

The children burst into laughter, their joy bouncing off the kitchen walls. Sarah, smiling warmly, lifted them up with gentle hands, her love for them evident in every touch.

Andrew appeared in the kitchen, his tie neatly fastened, his face bright with anticipation. "Morning!" he greeted, his smile genuine. "Is breakfast ready?"

"It is," Sarah replied, her gaze full of affection. She handed him a box of disposable cutlery, her hands moving deftly despite the tiredness in her eyes.

Andrew took the box and pulled out the last fork, nodding with a slight smile. He glanced at the trash where Sarah tossed the empty box, their lives marked by practical but loving routines.

Sitting down at the table, Andrew dug into the breakfast—a modest but lovingly prepared spread of pancakes and an omelet. "This is really good, thanks," he said, savoring the meal.

Sarah's smile faded slightly as she studied him. "Didn't you think about checking if there was a mistake with your bonus? Maybe they just made an error?"

Andrew sighed, his expression weary. "Sarah, I don't think—"

"Please, just look into it today," Sarah interjected, her tone a mix of concern and insistence. Her eyes were full of hope, reflecting her desire to improve their situation.

Andrew took a deep breath and nodded, giving in to her concern. "Alright, I'll check," he agreed, his voice softened by his love for her.

Sarah's face brightened with relief. She reached for an envelope on the counter and showed it to him. "I got this notice," she said, her voice steady but concerned. The envelope read: "MISSED THE SECOND NON-PAYMENT OF THE LOAN."

Andrew let out a frustrated sigh. "We'll get it sorted. I'll take the kids and talk to Matthew about it."

"Thanks," Sarah said, her gratitude evident. She tried to mask her anxiety but couldn't hide the worry in her eyes.

Andrew's mood visibly shifted, but he maintained his focus on their family. Despite their financial strain, their love for each other was unwavering.

"I'm going to see the soothsayer today," Sarah said, attempting to lighten the mood. "It's free for the first session."

Andrew raised an eyebrow in surprise. "Free?"

"Yeah," Sarah replied, a hint of amusement in her voice. "The first session's free, and if you go later, you pay for two."

Andrew chuckled softly, his affection for her apparent. "So, you're not planning on going back for more, are you?"

"Not yet," Sarah said with a playful grin, her eyes twinkling with a mixture of mischief and optimism.

After breakfast, Andrew prepared to leave. As he bent down to tie his shoelaces, he noticed Sarah's bright red toenails coming into view. He looked up to find her smiling at him.

"Got ten minutes?" Sarah asked, her voice gentle.

"Yeah, I've got time," Andrew replied with a laugh, the tension in his shoulders easing.

Sarah leaned in and kissed his cheek, a brief but tender gesture of support. She closed the door behind him, the sound echoing softly in their home—a place of love and mutual support.

—m—

Andrew stepped outside into the refreshing cool air of the morning. He closed his eyes, lifting his face to the gentle breeze as if to shake off the lingering shadows of the night. He took a deep breath, letting the crisp air fill his lungs, and slowly exhaled, feeling a sense of calm wash over him. The simple pleasure of the morning air seemed to clear his mind, pushing away the troubling fragments of a recent nightmare and the troubling thoughts about his estranged father.

He opened his eyes, focusing on the present as he walked towards his car. The old sedan—its paint chipped and faded, its bumper dented, but it was reliable enough for his needs.

He took another deep breath, reminding himself of the positives in his life—the support of his wife, the laughter of his children, and the small victories that made the daily grind bearable. The nightmare of the night before, filled with haunting memories and fears of his father, seemed to fade as he immersed himself in the routine of starting a new day..

As Andrew opened the car door, the sound of a harsh, ragged cough interrupted the quiet morning. He turned to see an old man leaning against the wall, dressed in tattered, filthy clothes. The man's hands were wrapped in dirty bandages, and his nails were caked with grime. He looked as though he were barely holding on, his gaze fixed on Andrew with a mix of desperation and hope.

"I'm sorry... What's your name?" the old man rasped, his voice barely audible.

"Andrew," he replied, his voice curt and guarded.

The old man's eyes flickered with a glimmer of hope. "And what about your salary?" he asked, his voice trembling with a mix of fear and desperation.

Andrew glanced at the old man but quickly turned away, his face showing a blend of annoyance and discomfort. He focused on opening the car door of his old, beat-up sedan, ignoring the stranger.

"I'm not a beggar!" the old man croaked, his plea coming out weak and strained. His voice cracked with desperation, trying to make himself heard.

Ignoring the old man's continued entreaties, Andrew shoved the car door open.

"Andrew!" the old man called out, his voice breaking. "Don't worry about the money! It will come! Just keep working! Keep going..."

Sarah's anxious voice cut through the air as she hurried over. "Andrew!" she called, her concern evident as she approached.

Seeing Sarah, Andrew attempted to brush past the old man, who continued to mumble, "Keep working! The money will come! It always does..."

With a frustrated shove, Andrew pushed the old man, who fell to the ground, his fear evident as he scrambled back. "Get out of here!" Andrew snapped, his irritation clear.

The old man, visibly shaken, scrambled away, his eyes wide with fear and confusion.

Sarah, her face pale with worry, quickly ushered the children into the car. She stood beside Andrew, her concern palpable. "Who was that?" she asked, her voice trembling slightly.

"Just some crazy guy," Andrew replied, trying to sound dismissive. But his eyes betrayed a hint of unease.

Sarah gently took Andrew's hand, guiding him toward the car. As they stood by the open door, she looked at him with growing concern. "Do you think he might have been... your father?" she asked cautiously.

Andrew's face tightened. A flicker of pain crossed his features before he forced a strained laugh. "No... no way," he said, trying to brush it off with a forced joke. "He'd have been rotting in a gutter for years."

Sarah's eyes remained troubled as she searched his face. "Are you sure?"

"Yes," Andrew said, forcing a reassuring smile that didn't quite reach his eyes.

Sarah offered a small, worried smile in return and climbed into the car. The couple, with their children, settled into the old sedan and drove off..

—⁂—

"Hello! How are you?" Matthew greeted the Browns with a warm smile, his voice echoing slightly in the spacious living room.

"Hey, Matthew," Andrew replied, shaking hands with his friend. The walls of Matthew's home were adorned with various memorabilia, old photographs, and quirky decorations, giving the place a cozy, lived-in feel. The children, already familiar with Matthew's place, eagerly rushed into the cluttered back room where he kept old things.

"Listen, do you still have our old instruments?" Andrew asked, his curiosity piqued as he glanced around the room filled with nostalgic clutter.

"Yeah, they're around here somewhere. Why?" Matthew replied, leading them through a narrow hallway lined with framed posters and vintage knick-knacks.

"Let the kids play with them. They'll love it," Andrew suggested.

Matthew smiled approvingly and nodded. "We'll be back by six," Andrew added, turning to leave.

Sarah, sensing an opportunity, gave her husband a meaningful look. Andrew stopped, glanced at her, and then turned back to Matthew. "Do you have any plans for tonight?"

"Want to meet with the producer?" Matthew asked, catching on quickly.

"Yeah, do you think we can make it today?" Andrew replied, the hope evident in his voice.

"I'll call them," Matthew said with a reassuring nod.

"Great." Andrew turned back to Sarah, who smiled in satisfaction.

"Good luck!" Matthew wished them as they left, his voice trailing off as the front door closed behind them.

As they drove off, Noah's indignant voice echoed from inside, "Uncle Matthew! Where are our toys?!"

Matthew laughed, looking guilty. "I'll get you something better," he promised. He headed to the pantry and began rummaging through an old, dusty box, while the children waited eagerly in the dimly lit room.

"Here we go!" Matthew said triumphantly, emerging with the box.

"What is it?" Renee asked, her eyes wide with curiosity.

Matthew carefully wiped off the dust and placed it in front of the children. "When your dad and I were kids, a little older than you, we used to play with this," he explained.

The children's eyes widened in surprise as they peered inside. The box contained various musical instruments: electronic keys, a flute, a homemade ukulele, and other old treasures.

"Oh, it's Mom!" Noah exclaimed, noticing a photo among the instruments.

"And this is Daddy and Uncle Matthew!" Renee added excitedly.

"Do you see Mom's tummy?" Matthew asked Noah, who nodded obediently. "Can you imagine you were in your mom's tummy then?"

Noah and Renee burst into laughter. "Was I that small?" Noah asked.

"And me?" his sister echoed.

"Everyone used to be like that," Matthew explained with a chuckle.

Noah picked up the flute and began to play, making a joyful noise. Renee continued to stare at the photo, captivated by the glimpse into the past.

"When was that?" she asked, her voice filled with wonder.

"At Mom and Dad's wedding," Matthew replied, his eyes softening at the memory.

"Wow!" Renee said dreamily.

Noah handed the flute to his sister and took out the ukulele. For the children, the room transformed into a grand theater, and they were the main orchestra. Matthew watched them with a fond smile, the chaotic harmony of brother and sister filling the room with life and laughter.

"Are you really getting married?" Matthew asked, disbelief coloring his voice as he sank into the lone chair in his new apartment.

"Yeah," Andrew sighed, still in shock himself. "We've already talked to her parents, found a pastor, invited people."

Matthew let out a chuckle, shaking his head. "You haven't even been dating for a year! Do you even love her?"

Andrew paused, his expression thoughtful. "Yeah, I do," he said quietly.

"And what about Grace?" Matthew probed. "Don't you like her too?"

Andrew's face fell a bit, a hint of sadness creeping in. "She's not pregnant with my child, is she?"

Matthew nodded, understanding the situation. He glanced around the nearly empty apartment. It was new, barely furnished with just a few boxes, a mattress on the floor, and a guitar leaning in the corner.

"So," Matthew said, breaking the silence, "I guess this is our grand bachelor party, huh?"

Andrew laughed. "Looks like it."

Matthew slapped the mattress playfully. "Here's to you and Sarah then!" He handed Andrew a bottle.

They clinked bottles, sharing a moment of camaraderie.

"Have you become a family man already, buying non-alcoholic beer?" Matthew teased, smirking.

Andrew glanced down, absentmindedly tracing the scar on his hand. His smile faded a little.

"Are you afraid of becoming like your father?" Matthew asked seriously, breaking the playful mood.

Andrew winced. "No," he said with a touch of pain in his voice. "I'm just trying to save for the wedding and then I need to find an apartment..."

Matthew put a reassuring hand on his friend's shoulder. "Andrew, I'll help as much as I can. Don't worry."

Andrew managed a grateful smile. "Well, then, here's to you too!" He raised his bottle for another toast.

"Yeah, and then we'll smoke some tea," Matthew joked, lightening the mood again.

They both laughed, the sound filling the small apartment, a brief respite from the weight of the future looming over Andrew.

—∞—

"Be sure to ask about your bonus," Sarah said, her voice tinged with hope as she looked at her husband.

"Okay," Andrew replied, his tone distant. He handed the car keys to Sarah.

Taking the keys, Sarah hesitated before saying, "I'm going to the fortune teller now. Do you want me to ask something for you?"

Andrew sighed. "Ask if working with a producer is the right decision for me," he said skeptically.

Sarah leaned over and kissed him on the cheek. "I will." With that, Andrew got out of the car and headed to work while Sarah drove off to her appointment.

As Sarah navigated through the rundown part of town, an uneasy feeling settled in her stomach. The neighborhood was filled with dilapidated buildings and graffiti-covered walls. She double-checked the address, her eyes darting nervously around the area. Finally, she spotted a small, inconspicuous sign that read "Madame Fate." Taking a deep breath, she approached the door beneath the sign, her hand trembling slightly as she gripped the handle and pushed it open.

A stone staircase descended into darkness, sending a shiver down her spine. "Come on, Sarah, you have to do this. You need answers," she whispered to herself. With another deep breath, she stepped into the gloom.

At the bottom of the stairs, she found a corridor decorated with various cryptic symbols and pictures. She barely understood their meanings, but they added to the eerie atmosphere. She continued until she reached a room draped in heavy, dark curtains. The air was thick with the smell of incense and herbs, making her eyes water. In the center of the room was a small round table with a book and a tea set.

"Apparently someone is a tea lover," Sarah thought wryly, trying to calm her nerves. Her attention was drawn by a soft cough to her left. A woman sat in a high-backed chair, her red lips curving into a smile as she gazed at Sarah.

"Welcome, Sarah," the woman said, her voice silky yet unsettling.

Sarah stared in amazement. How did she know her name? "You left a message, remember?" the woman added, her voice soothing.

"Oh, right. I must have forgotten," Sarah said awkwardly, trying to recall.

"Sit down, please," the woman continued. "I'm Shyla. You have a happy life, don't you? A good friend, perhaps?"

"Grace?" Sarah thought, but quickly pushed the painful memory aside. "It doesn't matter," she said, sitting down.

Shyla moved to a large, antique chest of drawers filled with numerous compartments. She opened the farthest drawer and retrieved a small bottle of liquid and a couple of wooden sticks. Returning to the table, she looked at Sarah intently.

"What's troubling you? What questions do you have?" Shyla asked.

"I'm interested in…"

"Remember, I'll answer only three questions in the first session, with a brief interpretation. After that, you'll need to pay," Shyla explained sternly.

Sarah hesitated, pondering the visit. Was this worth it, or was she being scammed? "Don't worry, you'll get answers," Shyla assured her. "Now, let's begin. You have financial problems, right?"

"Yes," Sarah replied uncertainly. "My husband wants to sign a contract, but it doesn't guarantee success. Should he agree to it?"

"Give me your hand and focus on your husband and his job," Shyla instructed.

Taking Sarah's hand, Shyla closed her eyes and tilted her head back, her eyes moving beneath her lids. "So, you didn't get married for love," Shyla said, peeking at Sarah.

"Not for love? We really care about each other. We have two children," Sarah protested.

"Perhaps the feelings developed over time," Shyla shrugged. "I see great success and wealth from this contract, but something blocks the full picture…"

Sarah felt a mix of relief and skepticism. She hoped Shyla's predictions were true. Shyla opened the bottle and took Sarah's hand again. Before Sarah realized what was happening, a sharp pain shot through her palm. Blood pooled in her hand.

"What are you doing?!" Sarah cried, clutching her hand to her chest.

"Relax. It's part of the ritual. Just a little bit of blood," Shyla said calmly. "You need answers, don't you?"

Sarah nodded reluctantly, opening her hand again. Shyla collected the blood, mixing it with the liquid in the bottle until it turned burgundy. She waved an incense stick over the bottle, then poured some of the liquid into her eyes. Her eyes turned a haunting red as she stared at Sarah.

"I sense a mysterious energy… It's faint, but it's there. Your ancestors protected you from karma, giving you a destined happy life. But something is interfering…" Shyla said, puzzled. "Do you have a picture of your husband?"

Sarah pulled a small photo from her purse and handed it over. "There's a strange aura around him. But he's not the source. It's a shadow behind him, waiting… But your husband protects it."

Sarah felt a chill. She wanted answers, not more questions. "This morning, an old man approached us. Who was he?" she asked.

"I don't see an old man, only a man in his prime with great energy," Shyla replied.

"That's strange…" Sarah thought, remembering the old man's eyes. They seemed familiar.

"What should we do about the shadow?" Sarah asked.

"I'll look into it and let you know what I find," Shyla said thoughtfully.

Sarah shifted uncomfortably in her seat, her initial intentions resurfacing. "Actually, I originally came here to ask about myself and my family. But somehow, I ended up asking about my husband," she admitted.

Shyla's eyes gleamed with a knowing look. "Nothing happens accidentally, dear. Now you know about the shadow, and it is linked to your husband. Everything is interconnected."

Sarah left the fortune teller's room with mixed feelings. She thanked Shyla and walked out, her mind swirling with uncertainty and fear for what the future might hold.

—∞—

At the end of a long working day and after purchasing various groceries, Sarah arrived to pick up her husband. She parked their old, damaged car in the lot and settled in, trying to get comfortable in the worn-out seat. The monotony of waiting created various inconveniences. Leaning her hand on the steering wheel, Sarah was preoccupied with the sharp burning pain in her left palm. The wound from the soothsayer earlier that day gnawed at her thoughts, the thin, deep cut a constant reminder of the unsettling ritual.

"Hi," Andrew said as he opened the car door, his voice carrying a forced cheerfulness.

Sarah looked up from her hand and turned to her husband. "Promotion?" she asked cautiously, her hope evident.

Andrew's smile was wide but seemed slightly strained. "Yes! They gave me a promotion! The car is ours!" he announced with an enthusiasm that seemed to falter slightly at the edges.

Sarah laughed, a genuine sound of relief and joy. "I'm so glad! What a relief," she said, wrapping her arms around him in a heartfelt hug. They shared a smile, but Sarah's mind was still partly on the unsettling events of the day.

After the embrace, Sarah's excitement continued. "Well? Now for the other good news?"

Andrew's face shifted to a puzzled expression. "What do you mean?" he asked, the confusion clear in his tone.

Sarah's smile widened as she responded, "Well, did Matthew get in touch with the producer? I hope he has some good news there too."

Andrew's expression clouded briefly. He looked away, a hint of discomfort in his eyes. "Ah... I thought you meant children."

Sarah noticed the slight shift in Andrew's demeanor. "Well, yes, the children and Matthew and the producer are all good news," she said, her voice light as she started the car and pulled away from the parking lot.

Andrew's gaze lingered on the road ahead, his thoughts evidently preoccupied. "Yes..." he said, a thoughtful tone in his voice that hinted at something more. His eyes betrayed a flicker of unease, as if Sarah's mention of Matthew and the producer struck a nerve.

The ride to Mathew's was quiet, each lost in their own thoughts. Sarah couldn't shake the eerie feeling from her visit to the fortune teller. She glanced at her wounded palm again, the pain a constant reminder. The old car jolted over a bump, and Sarah glanced at Andrew, noting the tension in his posture. "You know," she began, trying to sound casual, "I asked the fortune teller about you today, but I originally went there to ask about myself and our family."

Andrew's curiosity was piqued, but his face remained guarded. "Really? What did she say?"

Sarah hesitated, the memory of the soothsayer's cryptic words swirling in her mind. "She mentioned that nothing happens by accident, that everything is interconnected. And now we know about this shadow... It's unsettling."

Andrew's frown deepened slightly, his skepticism evident. "A shadow? What does that even mean?"

"I'm not sure," Sarah admitted, her voice tinged with concern. "But she seemed to think it was important. We need to be cautious."

Andrew's reaction was a mix of disbelief and something more complex—perhaps jealousy or frustration. "We'll figure it out, Sarah," he said, his tone more resolute than convinced. "Together."

—ɷ—

"Mom! Dad! Look!" Noah's voice rang out, his excitement palpable as he held up a drawing.

Sarah glanced at Andrew, her eyes urging him to engage with their son while she savored the quiet evening.

"What's this you've got there, buddy?" Andrew asked, leaning over the drawing with an exaggerated concentration.

Noah's face beamed with pride.

"Mom's in a pretty dress," he said, pointing to a figure.

"That's right!" Sarah said, her smile broadening.

"And I'm holding Rene," Andrew continued, studying the drawing closely.

"Yes!" Noah confirmed enthusiastically.

"And where are you in this picture?" Andrew asked, trying to keep his tone light.

Noah giggled and pointed to a small house in the background.

"That's where I am! Uncle Matthew tells me stories there!" he explained, his voice full of joy.

Andrew's expression tightened slightly. The image of Matthew with Noah stirred an unsettling feeling. His son seemed to place Matthew in a role Andrew felt he should occupy himself.

"Noah, remember, family is the most important thing," Andrew said firmly, his voice carrying an edge of frustration.

"But Uncle Matthew is family, too," Noah replied, his innocence clear.

"Matthew isn't part of our family like we are," Andrew interrupted, his tone sharper than intended.

A hush fell over the room. Sarah and Matthew exchanged uneasy glances. The distant sounds of Rene playing in the next room filled the silence. Andrew, feeling the weight of the moment, stood up abruptly and took Noah's hand.

"Let's go find your sister," Andrew said, his voice more authoritative than before.

As they walked towards the nursery, Andrew's mind churned with worry. His financial struggles gnawed at him. The promotion he'd fabricated was meant to ease Sarah's concerns, but the truth was far bleaker. The constant financial strain was eroding his sense of self-worth.

In the nursery, Andrew smiled at Rene, who was strumming a small ukulele.

"Ready for bed, sweetheart?" Andrew asked gently.

Rene's eyes widened in protest.

"No! I don't want to!" she declared.

Andrew laughed softly and scooped her up.

"Come on, let's go. I'll play something special for you," he promised, trying to lift the mood.

The children settled into bed, their anticipation visible. Andrew retrieved the old guitar from Matthew's closet, his movements deliberate. As he tuned the strings, he focused intently, finding solace in the familiar routine.

"Bravo!" Rene clapped as Andrew began to play.

Andrew's fingers glided over the strings, creating a soft, soothing melody. The music seemed to envelop him, and he felt himself slipping into a state of serene escape. The melody became a refuge from his anxieties, a space where he could momentarily forget the mounting pressures of his life. His eyes closed, and his entire being seemed to merge with the guitar. The notes flowed effortlessly, each strum bringing a sense of calm and release.

As Andrew played, the music seemed to transcend the room, creating a bubble of tranquility around him. The children's steady breathing and the gentle strumming created a lullaby that felt almost magical. Andrew's thoughts drifted away from his worries about money and the strained relationship with Sarah and Matthew. The guitar became his sanctuary, a place where he could lose himself in pure, untroubled bliss.

After the children had fallen asleep, Andrew placed the guitar back in the closet, his mind still floating in the afterglow of his musical escape. He returned to the kitchen, where Sarah and Matthew were engaged in a discussion.

"Missed it?" Matthew asked, a smirk playing at the corners of his mouth.

Andrew nodded, a dreamy expression still on his face.

"Yeah," he replied, his voice carrying a hint of reverie.

Sarah looked at him with warm admiration, but Andrew couldn't shake the feeling that she saw more value in Matthew's presence than in his own. The financial strain and Matthew's seeming stability were a constant source of tension. Andrew couldn't ignore the gnawing sense of inadequacy, particularly as he observed Sarah's easy interaction with Matthew.

"The kids are asleep," Andrew announced, sitting down at the table.

Sarah stood up and gently touched Andrew's shoulders before heading back to the children. Matthew's eyes followed her, a shadow of something inscrutable crossing his face.

Andrew's mind raced as he prepared to address Matthew.

"Listen... I didn't actually get the promotion," Andrew began, his voice hesitant.

Matthew's eyebrows raised in surprise.

"Oh? What happened?" he asked, curiosity laced with concern.

Andrew sighed deeply, looking away.

"The presentation went well, but there was no bonus. I told Sarah there was a promotion to keep her spirits up," he confessed, guilt evident in his tone.

"Why lie about it?" Matthew inquired, his voice gentle but probing.

"She's worried about money. We're barely making ends meet," Andrew explained. "We've even had to borrow water from neighbors, and today we got a warning about the car loan. It's been tough with the kids' education and everything else. Sarah constantly reminds me of our financial problems. I thought a lie might help ease her burden, even if just for a little while."

Matthew listened attentively, his expression thoughtful. The gravity of Andrew's situation was clear.

"Did you talk to the producer?" Andrew asked, trying to shift the focus.

Matthew nodded slowly.

"Yes, he's in town until 4 am. We can go see him if you're ready."

"I'll tell Sarah we're heading out," Andrew said, rising from his chair.

Sarah entered the room just then, her curiosity piqued.

"Where are you going?" she asked, her voice tinged with concern.

Andrew approached her, wrapping her in a reassuring hug.

"I'm going to celebrate the promotion," he said, forcing a cheerful tone.

Sarah looked at him, puzzled.

"Are you sure? What about the producer?" she asked, trying to mask her anxiety about their finances.

"Yes, we'll handle it. I'll probably be out for a while," Andrew said, attempting to sound confident.

Sarah embraced him, her confusion evident.

"All right. Take care of things and come home soon," she said softly.

"I will," Andrew replied, his smile hiding his inner turmoil as he went to get the children.

—∞—

The old car crept to a stop in the opulent parking lot of a high-end club, its rusted exterior glaringly out of place among the sleek, expensive vehicles. Inside, Andrew and Matthew sat in the worn seats, their anxiety palpable.

Andrew's mind was clouded with thoughts of mounting debts, a lie he'd told Sarah, and the unrelenting pressure to provide for his family.

He glanced at the meager amount of cash he had, barely enough to cover tonight's expenses. Meanwhile, Matthew was preoccupied with his appearance, his nerves frayed as he checked his bank balance. The figure was disheartening—just under a thousand dollars.

"Andrew?" Matthew asked, his voice tinged with anxiety. "How much do we have for tonight?"

Andrew's expression was blank as he replied.

"No more than a hundred."

Matthew's fingers drummed nervously on his knees, his face betraying his concern.

"This producer is a big deal. One moment he's your best friend, the next he's dismissing you like you're nothing. We should have come better prepared."

Andrew's tone was firm but weighed down with stress.

"Matthew, this meeting is crucial. I can't pay my bills, I'm in debt, and I need to support my family. I'm not here to play games."

Matthew nodded, acknowledging the seriousness of Andrew's situation. They both stepped out of the car and approached the entrance of the club.

A burly bouncer, his expression hard and dismissive, blocked their path.

"What's the occasion?" he grunted.

"We're here for the club," Andrew replied, trying to sound assertive.

"Not with that car, you're not. Move along."

Matthew interjected with a touch of desperation.

"We're supposed to meet Bradley Belfort."

The bouncer's demeanor changed abruptly. His face softened into an apologetic smile.

"My apologies, Mr. Brown. Please, come right in. Would you like you car washed?"

"Uh, no need for car washing," Andrew said, still trying to grasp the sudden shift in attitude.

"It's complimentary," the bouncer assured.

Andrew and Matthew exchanged incredulous glances as they entered the club, their confusion palpable.

Inside, the club was a sensory overload. The music pounded with relentless intensity, mingling with the raucous laughter and the haze of smoke. The air was thick with the scent of expensive perfumes and a hint of something more illicit. Women in provocative outfits glided by, their every move dripping with sensuality, while men in tailored suits flaunted their wealth.

A stunning woman with an air of effortless seduction approached them. Her eyes sparkled with mischief, and her figure was a perfect blend of allure and sophistication.

"Hello, gentlemen," she purred, her voice like silk. "I'm Lilith. Mr. Belfort is expecting you."

Matthew's gaze lingered on Lilith, captivated by her beauty and poise. Andrew, however, was absorbed in the opulence of the surroundings, the stark contrast to his own financial struggles making his stomach churn.

They followed Lilith through the club, her presence both mesmerizing and unsettling. The room they entered was a showcase of excess. Mr.

Belfort lounged on a plush burgundy sofa, surrounded by four equally stunning women. The table was laden with dishes and drinks so extravagant that they might as well have been from another world. The sheer display of wealth was overwhelming.

"Have a seat, gentlemen," Mr. Belfort said, gesturing grandly with his cigar.

Andrew and Matthew sat down, their discomfort evident.

"Dance for now, ladies," Mr. Belfort commanded, dismissing the women with a wave. He then turned his attention to his guests. "So, what brings you here?"

Matthew cleared his throat, his confidence wavering.

"My name is Matthew, and this is Andrew. We've known each other since we were kids, and we both have a deep appreciation for music…"

"Connoisseurs, then?" Mr. Belfort interrupted, blowing a cloud of smoke with a smirk.

"Yes," Matthew replied, his throat dry. "We have some old recordings we'd like you to hear…"

Mr. Belfort raised a hand, signaling for silence.

"I've heard your recordings," he said dismissively.

Andrew and Matthew exchanged startled looks.

"So, what's your take?" Andrew asked, his voice tinged with hope.

Mr. Belfort scrutinized Andrew with a penetrating gaze, his glasses slipping down his nose.

"I evaluate my potential projects with great care," he said, his tone as cold as the ice in his drink. "Your music has potential, but I'm interested in more than that. Do you have charisma? Can you perform? Can you captivate an audience?"

Andrew and Matthew's enthusiasm dimmed.

"That's why we're here," Matthew said, forcing a smile. "We're ready to do whatever it takes."

Mr. Belfort's demeanor shifted to one of mock enthusiasm.

"Drink something, take something, sniff something, smoke something—I don't care. Just show me what you've got," he said with a dismissive wave.

The friends laughed nervously, the pressure mounting.

"AAAGH! HAHAHA!" Mr. Belfort suddenly roared, slapping his knee. "Finally, the pill's working after all! Lilith!"

Lilith returned with a procession of other women, each carrying vials and bottles filled with various substances. The scene was surreal and intoxicating. Andrew's eyes darted around, taking in the hedonistic display of wealth and excess. He glanced at his wedding ring, then at the beautiful women surrounding them, his internal struggle laid bare.

"Here you go, darling," Lilith said, handing Andrew a glass of whiskey with a delicate twist of ice.

Mr. Belfort raised his glass in a toast, his smile twisted with satisfaction.

"To you!" he said, his eyes gleaming with a devilish delight.

Andrew took a deep breath and downed the drink. Thus the fun began.

—◊—

The laughter of girls, the clinking of glasses, and the intoxicating atmosphere of the club had left Andrew in a dizzying state of euphoria. The night had been a blur of seductive smiles, music that thumped in his chest, and the haze of pills that had distorted reality. The effects of the drugs were potent—his senses were heightened, yet detached, making everything seem both vivid and surreal. Every touch felt electric, every glance from Lilith a spark in his already heightened state. She had been close all evening, her warm, perfumed skin brushing against him as she whispered flirtatious promises.

Lilith. Her beauty was beyond anything Andrew had ever seen, more captivating than any image he'd ever glimpsed on screen. She had been by his side all night, her touch both alluring and disorienting. He found himself fixated on the rising bubbles in her glass of champagne, each bubble sparkling like tiny coins, shimmering with the promise of wealth.

The bubbles in Lilith's champagne seemed to dance with a life of their own, each one a tiny glimmer of gold. Andrew's gaze followed them, his mind racing with the thought of wealth and opulence. He wondered if he could ever live the life of luxury that he had witnessed tonight— where money flowed like the champagne and people seemed to have no worries beyond the next thrill. The rich talked about their values, yet Andrew knew that for him, money was not just a value—it was a necessity. The constant weight of debt and the looming bills for his children's future were a stark contrast to the freedom he glimpsed tonight.

The pills had made him feel invincible, yet emotionally raw. Every sensation was amplified—the touch of the women, the music that felt like it was wrapped around him, and the almost unbearable urge to escape his reality. His mind drifted in and out of focus, the world around him shifting like a dream.

After a round of toasts and a few more pills discreetly slipped into his drinks, the high reached its peak. Andrew felt an exhilarating rush, but also a deep, gnawing dissatisfaction.

"Money," he thought hazily. "It's always about money. The rich speak of values and ideals, but they forget what it's like to struggle, to worry about the next meal or paying for school. I have a wife, kids. We're barely scraping by, living on loans... Money, I need it. I need him to sign us."

As the final toast was made, the room was filled with a mix of drunken cheers and seductive whispers. The women flirted shamelessly, their voices hushed and sultry. The producer, a smirk playing at the corners of his lips, made his farewell.

"There'll be a car waiting for you at the exit. It will take you wherever you need," he said with a grin.

"Thank you!" Andrew and Matthew slurred, their speech thick with alcohol.

Lilith stood, her movements fluid and graceful. She slid her hand up Andrew's chest to his shoulder, her touch lingering before she pressed a soft kiss to his cheek. Andrew was torn between feeling repulsed and mesmerized. The confusion was palpable.

Guided by Lilith, the men were ushered out of the club and into a sleek black limousine. The car's opulence contrasted sharply with the dilapidated state of Andrew's old car.

"So, what do you think?" Matthew asked, a goofy grin plastered on his face.

"This is amazing!" Andrew shouted, raising his hands in exhilaration.

The friends laughed and shared their impressions of the evening, their voices echoing in the lavish interior of the limousine. Time slipped away unnoticed as they reveled in their unexpected stroke of luck. The limo came to a stop outside Andrew's apartment.

"Already?" Matthew asked, a note of disbelief in his voice.

"I didn't even realize," Andrew replied, stepping out of the car. "Alright, see you later!"

"See you!" Matthew waved, his gesture enthusiastic but unsteady.

Andrew closed the door and inhaled the cool night air. The intoxicating blend of alcohol and adrenaline buzzed through him, and he felt a strange sense of disconnection from reality.

"Andrew..." a hoarse voice called out from the darkness.

"Huh?" Andrew muttered, his vision swimming as he tried to locate the source of the voice.

"Andrew..."

The voice was old and ragged, and it carried with it a weight of unfulfilled rage. Andrew's anger surged, an uncontrollable torrent of resentment and frustration.

"Where the hell are you?! I know who you are!!! Don't come near me! You killed my mother! You left me! Go screw yourself, you worthless old man!" Andrew shouted, his voice cracking with raw emotion.

"Andrew!!!" The voice grew louder, more insistent.

"What the hell do you want from me?! Are you dead? Are you calling me from hell as a ghost? Should I kill myself to fight you in hell? That's how much I hate you!"

He was overcome by a fit of rage, his breathing ragged as he collapsed to the ground. The anger and desperation seemed to drain from him, leaving only exhaustion and a twisted sense of irony.

"Look at me... A grown man still crying about my father. If it's really you from hell, I can't give you anything. You took everything from me. All I have is a painful reminder of your brutality. If you're really calling my name, then give me back what you took. Give me the life I want."

He stood, shaking, and staggered toward his apartment, the dim light from the hallway flickering against his face. As he entered his apartment, the stark reality of his situation hit him again. The worn furniture, the peeling paint, and the oppressive sense of poverty were suffocating.

The apartment was a constant reminder of his failures. Andrew's gaze fell on the dingy surroundings, each detail a stark contrast to the opulence he had glimpsed earlier. The small, shabby room seemed more unbearable than ever, and his own reflection in the grimy mirror was a painful reminder of his situation.

Andrew stumbled into his bedroom, his anger morphing into a deep-seated disgust. He threw his clothes aside with violent gestures, the filth and clutter of the apartment seeming to mock him. He lay back on the bed, the drugs making his thoughts drift in and out of focus. The small, dingy room seemed to close in on him, the shadows of his own inadequacy pressing down.

In his intoxicated haze, Andrew's gaze was drawn to the stark contrast between his own meager existence and the luxurious life he had briefly tasted. The memory of Lilith's touch and the opulence of the club lingered, fueling a deep-seated frustration. He closed his eyes, but the anger towards his father and the overwhelming sense of failure remained. The night's debauchery had been a fleeting escape, but now, faced with the stark reality of his life, Andrew's thoughts turned darker. The whispered promises of wealth and happiness seemed more distant than ever, swallowed by the grim confines of his impoverished existence.

As he drifted into a restless sleep, the echoes of the night's events haunted him—an unfulfilled longing for a life he could barely imagine, and a deep, unrelenting rage that continued to fester.

—⚋—

"Hello, Mr. Brown," came a voice, cold and disembodied.

Andrew jolted awake in his own bedroom, but something was dreadfully wrong. Time felt suspended, as if it had ceased to exist altogether. An eerie, pervasive sense of dread clung to him, making the air feel thick and suffocating. He reached out to touch Sarah, but his hands seemed to pass through her, as if she were a ghost—or he himself had become one.

"Sarah, wake up!" Andrew shouted, panic lacing his voice.

"It's no use; she won't wake up," replied a calm, unfamiliar voice from across the room.

Andrew's heart raced. He turned, his body freezing as he saw a man seated in the chair opposite the bed. Fear gripped him, turning his hands icy cold and raising goosebumps on his skin.

"Who are you?! What are you doing here?!" Andrew demanded, his voice trembling as he tried to rouse his wife. "Sarah! Sarah!"

With a burst of adrenaline, Andrew leaped at the stranger, fists clenched. But the man raised his palm, and Andrew froze mid-air, suspended by an invisible force.

"What is happening?! Who are you?!" Andrew yelled, struggling to move.

"Calm down..." The man's voice was smooth, almost mocking.

"Get out of here!" Andrew's shout was desperate.

The stranger waved his fingers, and Andrew's mouth snapped shut with a sharp, painful click. The sound was like a heavy door slamming shut. Andrew's jaw clenched painfully, and his attempts to speak were futile. His fear spiraled, growing more intense.

"Sarah... What happened to her?! Is she alive? What about the children?" Andrew's frantic thoughts raced.

"Relax. She's fine, and your children too. I mean no harm to your family... yet," the man said, his tone dripping with menace.

"Yet?!" Andrew tried to scream, but the sound was muffled. His frustration grew as the stranger's patience wore thin. With another swift motion, the man twisted Andrew's tongue, sealing his throat and leaving him only able to breathe through his nose.

"You people are ridiculous," the man said with a hint of disgust. "You ask questions without thinking, react with violence at the slightest threat. Tell me, Andrew, would it really matter if I were the Devil himself? No. You are desperate, aren't you? You've called for help, haven't you? Ask the right questions, think before you speak. Though it's all the same to me."

Andrew's eyes widened in terror as a profound sense of emptiness washed over him. It was as if his heart had stopped, leaving him hollow and numb, a living corpse.

"You needn't fear me, nor should you call for Jesus," the man said with a chilling smile. "Calm yourself..." He commanded with an unsettling authority.

In an instant, the fear evaporated, replaced by a strange, unnatural calm. Andrew's mouth opened, and he took in a deep breath, feeling an almost serene clarity. He sat down slowly, trying to comprehend the surreal situation.

"What..." he began to ask.

"No! Think before you speak. Sarah is alright, your children too..." the man interrupted. "What questions do you need answers to? Who am I? What do I want from you? You summoned me, didn't you?"

Andrew's thoughts scrambled. "Money is the main issue... everything else is secondary," he considered.

"Ah, money," the man said, leaning forward with a predatory grin. "How much do you want? And what will you give in return?"

"How much can you give? What do you want?" Andrew asked, his voice steady but filled with underlying desperation.

"Name any amount, and I will provide it. Though I doubt money is the root of all your problems..." The man's gaze drifted to Sarah. "Do you truly love her?"

"Of course," Andrew thought instinctively.

"Then why not confess the nightmares that plague you? Why lie about your job? Why the fear that she might leave you for Matthew? Is this your definition of love?" The man's voice was penetrating, as if reading Andrew's soul.

Confusion clouded Andrew's mind. The man before him seemed beyond mortal, an otherworldly entity. He questioned his own sanity. "Who is this man? Can he be harmed?"

"Wrong questions again," the man said dismissively. "What is it that you truly desire? You don't love your family as you wished to. Why is that? Did you force yourself to love Sarah? Just as you forced yourself to love your father? Who did you love before? Who was the wife you envisioned?"

"Grace..." the thought flashed through Andrew's mind.

"Grace," the stranger repeated with an intrigued smile. "Is she the one you crave? I can help with that as well..." he suggested.

Andrew imagined a life with Grace—how she would care for him, how she would understand him, and how she could make him truly happy. The thought was intoxicating.

"So it's not that simple..." the man said. "Do you even know what you want?" he taunted.

"Can you stop the nightmares?" Andrew asked, clutching at a thread of hope.

"The nightmares with your father... Are you sure they're preventing you from what you want? Have you considered they might be shaping you into a better father, a loyal husband, even if not loving?" The man's tone was almost thoughtful.

Andrew was at a loss for words, overwhelmed by the complexity of his own thoughts.

"What do I want?" he finally asked, looking at the man with newfound clarity.

"You tell me. I am not here to preach, only to assist. But be aware, you are responsible for your choices," the man said with an inscrutable smile. "What is it that you desire?"

After a moment's contemplation, Andrew stood up with determination.

"I want the nightmares to stop. I want unimaginable wealth. And I want to stop being tormented by thoughts of my father."

"Very well," the Devil said with a pleased grin. "All I ask in return is that a part of me remains with you."

Andrew frowned. "A part of you? I don't even know you."

"You know who I am," the Devil said, rising from the chair. "You've always known."

"The Devil?" Andrew asked, his voice barely a whisper.

The Devil nodded. "You don't want a part of me?"

"You're already inside me," Andrew said quietly.

"Indeed. I've always been there. What stops you from controlling it further in your life?" The Devil's grin was predatory.

Andrew was silent, realizing for the first time how little he truly understood.

"I agree," Andrew said, finally resigning himself.

The Devil's smile widened, revealing perfect, gleaming teeth. He extended his hand.

Andrew took it, his grip steady.

"Excellent," the Devil said slyly. "When you wake, check your phone."

The Devil turned and lifted his hand, snapping his fingers. With a final, sinister smile, he vanished, leaving Andrew and his sleeping wife alone in the room.

The morning hangover hit Andrew with full force. He stroked Sarah to reassure himself that he was still in his body and went to wash his face. After his morning routine, he lay back down on the bed, trying to remember the dream he'd had. But it was elusive, slipping through his mind like sand. There was a lingering sense of expectation, though, but expectation of what? Or whom?

"Dear, turn off the alarm clock," Sarah mumbled, her voice thick with sleep as she reached for the ringing phone.

"Hello?" Andrew answered, rubbing his eyes.

"Andrew? This is Matthew. My phone's dead, so I'm calling from a friend's phone. How are you?"

"Oh, hey Matthew! Everything's fine. What's up?"

"Andrew, I have great news! We're accepted!!!"

"What?!" Andrew shouted, his excitement filling the entire apartment. He glanced over at Sarah.

"Let's go! I'll be waiting for you at the bar at 5 p.m. I'll meet the producer there," Matthew continued, his voice brimming with enthusiasm.

"Awesome!" Andrew said, ending the call and turning to Sarah.

"Well? What is it? Tell me!" Sarah asked eagerly, her eyes wide with anticipation.

"The producer!!! He signed us!" Andrew exclaimed, still in disbelief.

"Hurrah! Hurray! Hurrah!" Sarah cheered, her voice ringing with joy.

Both shared in the excitement, their happiness palpable.

"What's happening?" Noah came bounding into the room.

Andrew scooped up his son and said, "Your daddy will be signing for other people too!"

"Yay!" Noah yelled, his excitement matching his parents'.

"Wait... what?" Andrew stopped, a look of confusion crossing his face.

"What?" Sarah asked, her tone anxious.

Andrew pulled out his phone and stared at it in disbelief.

"Holy shit!!!" Andrew exclaimed. "I just got $25,000, as an invitation to perform at the Paradise Club!"

Sarah was speechless, overwhelmed by the sudden surge of joy.

"Daddy, you can't say that word, it's bad!" Rene chimed in, her small voice stern but playful.

Andrew laughed heartily. Overcome with joy, he picked up Rene too.

"Are we going to Uncle Matthew?" Noah asked, his face lit up with excitement.

Andrew smiled at his son and replied, "No. You're going to kindergarten now!"

Sarah looked at her husband with a mix of love and admiration. The whole family was on the brink of a new and exciting chapter in their lives.

CHAPTER

2

The dimly lit hall echoed with the muffled sounds of footsteps. A middle-aged man emerged from the shadows, moving with a smooth yet confident gait. His highly polished business shoes, gray sweater, and trousers gave him a classically simple appearance. But his proudly raised head, precise steps, and free movements exuded a sense of ownership over this infernal realm.

As he moved through the corridor, sounds seeping through the doors lining the hall interrupted the dead silence. The doors stood at different levels, each one exuding a unique aura of torment. Bitter, guttural crying came from one, manic laughter from another, and quiet screams from a third. The further he walked, the more varied and intense the sounds became, yet he continued with unwavering confidence. An elderly, unkempt man followed him modestly, his eyes darting nervously around the eerie hall.

"What kind of place is this?" the old man asked hoarsely, his voice trembling with fear.

"Your new home," the man replied, his voice smooth and unsettling.

After a while, the man stopped at one of the doors, inviting the old man to enter. The old man looked questioningly at the man and at the door, his heart pounding in his chest.

"What's there?" the old man asked, worried for his safety.

The man opened the door, revealing an ordinary, modest room, lit by a single old lamp, around which moths flew aimlessly. The walls were bare, and the air was thick with an unidentifiable scent that made the old man shiver.

"After you," the man invited him into the room.

The old man hesitantly entered and began to look around. The room had an old work table and a single bed, making it look more like a cell than a place of residence. Startled by the sharp sound of the door closing, the old man spun around, his eyes wide with fear.

"How old are you?" the man asked casually. "57," the old man replied obediently, his voice barely a whisper.

The man went to the worktable, opened a shelf, took out a vase of water, and handed it to the old man. The old man looked at the vase in confusion and then at the man, his hands trembling.

"Do you agree that life is the most valuable thing that can exist?" the man asked, looking into the old man's eyes with an intensity that made the old man uneasy. "Yes," he replied softly, clasping the vase as if it were a lifeline.

The man shifted his gaze from the old man to the room and began to examine it curiously.

"This room was made especially for you. Now it belongs entirely to you. You can leave anytime, enter anytime, and do anything in it," the man said. "You can do incredible things in this room. Here, your thoughts are transformed into reality through complex quantum events, tailored specifically for you. You control probability itself. In other words, the room is magical," he finished, his voice carrying an almost hypnotic quality.

The old man looked around the room in amazement, his eyes wide with disbelief.

"So I can imagine something, and it will appear here? In this room?" the old man asked, his voice trembling with excitement and fear. "That's right," the man replied. "Anything?" the old man asked, a childish smile spreading across his face. "Anything and anyone," the man repeated, his smile widening.

The old man began to imagine all the things he would do in the room, his mind racing with possibilities.

"Are there any consequences?" the old man asked uncertainly, his eyes flicking back to the man. "None," the man replied with a smile that didn't reach his eyes.

The old man imagined a thousand dollars on the desk, and they appeared. In surprise, he dropped the vase and ran to the table, frantically counting the bills. The man watched him curiously. The old man imagined two and a half million dollars, and an enormous pile of money formed in the center of the room. He laughed, throwing money in the air. The man watched him curiously, his eyes glinting with something dark.

The old man, giddy with power, imagined a trillion dollars, but they did not appear. He looked at the man questioningly and greedily.

"Only what fits in the room can appear here," the man clarified. "Ah," the old man said, understanding, and imagined a billion dollars, which appeared in smaller denominations scattered across the room.

After a while, he grew tired of the money and imagined a woman. A gorgeous woman of unearthly beauty appeared before him, her presence filling the room with an intoxicating scent. Her elegant, fitted dress clung to her curves before disappearing into thin air, revealing her flawless, naked figure. The old man smiled lasciviously, his breath quickening. The woman approached him, her movements slow and deliberate, her lips parting in a sultry smile. She kissed him passionately, her hands roaming over his body, and he groaned with pleasure.

The man looked at the old man disinterestedly and walked over to the vase on the floor. Bending down, he picked up the vase and placed it on the worktable next to the bills, to the sounds of the couple's rapid breathing. Examining the vase, the man created 57 roses in it, watching them wither and bloom repeatedly. Finally, leaving the roses in a fresh state, he turned towards the old man, who had completely forgotten about him. With a light movement of his hand, everything created by the old man disappeared. The old man desperately tried to hold onto the disappearing woman, convulsively trying to imagine her over and over again. He looked at the man in panic, as if he were his God.

"Give me back my abilities, please! I beg you!" the old man pleaded, falling to his knees.

"You'll have them when I leave the room," the man said, looking down at the worshiping old man and drawing his attention to the vase of flowers. "57 roses... Look after them. I will visit you periodically. See you later..."

The man turned around, opened the door, and left the room.

A dark blue sports car with a roaring engine sped past the glowing LOS ANGELES sign, its sleek curves glistening under the city lights. The interior was a symphony of luxury, with leather seats, a polished dashboard, and state-of-the-art controls that responded to the lightest touch. The cityscape blurred outside, a dazzling array of lights and colors.

"Listen, listen," Andrew said, his voice barely audible over the engine's growl. He was lounging in the driver's seat, his sunglasses perched on his nose despite the night. His designer clothes spoke of wealth, and his wristwatch, an exclusive limited edition, shimmered with understated elegance.

"Welcome to Grammy Live! My name is Mary Phillips, and I'm Rosalina Bridget. We are pleased to announce that the 67th Grammy Ceremony will begin in just a few hours! The greatest musicians and artists have already gathered on the red carpet in anticipation of the award! And here is our regular star. Please tell us your impressions when you learned about the next Grammy nomination..."

"I am incredibly grateful to all my listeners, family, and..."

"Blah, blah, blah..." Andrew muttered, pushing the car to its limits. The speedometer needle quivered near the top as they raced through the city, overtaking one car after another. The wind roared around them, filling the car with the sound of freedom.

"What are your thoughts on today's nominees?" the radio continued.

"I think it's worth celebrating the new artists in our ranks. Andrew and Matthew, an amazing album..."

"Thank you very much. Andrew and Matthew, just a few months ago, made a real splash all over the world with their debut album, taking first place in the world charts and winning the hearts of music fans..."

"Here's to us!" Matthew said, handing a pill to Andrew and swallowing one himself. Andrew followed suit, the pill's bitter taste lingering on his tongue.

The new Grammy nominees arrived on the red carpet ten minutes before the start of the ceremony. The roar of the dark blue car's engine drew the attention of photographers and celebrities alike. Andrew stepped out of the car, sunglasses shielding his eyes from the blinding flashes of cameras and the screams of adoring fans.

"Andrew! Andrew! I love you!" a voice cried out from somewhere in the crowd.

With his Hollywood smile, Andrew waved to his fans, signing autographs as he moved through the throng of people.

"Can I get an autograph? Sign on me!" a woman called out seductively, revealing her breasts.

Andrew hesitated for a moment before leaning in to write his autograph on the woman's chest. As he did, he felt his fingers grow numb, his motor functions slipping away. He laughed, a cough interrupting his mirth, and waved once more to his fans before heading to the red carpet.

"Mr. Brown! Mr. Brown!" the presenter's voice cut through the noise.

Andrew turned around, the world around him blurring. He felt a wave of disorientation wash over him.

"What are your expectations for tonight?" the presenter asked, her microphone thrust towards him.

Sniffing, Andrew pulled the microphone closer and looked into the camera. "I'm sorry, what did you ask?" he said, forgetting the question.

"What are your expectations?" the presenter repeated, leaning in closer.

"To please people..." Andrew replied, locking eyes with her and smiling.

"Andrew Brown, ladies and gentlemen!" the presenter announced to the camera.

"And it's off! We're done," the cameraman said, turning off the camera.

"Good luck to you," the presenter smiled at Andrew.

Andrew smiled back, his steps unsteady as he made his way to the ceremony. Lights, flashes, smiles, screams, music, blackouts—everything blurred together in his mind. He found himself in the bathroom, staring into the mirror. Not quite understanding what had happened, he decided to wash up. The sound of the toilet door opening made him tense. The girl who had recently interviewed him pushed him against the wall, her breath hot on his neck.

"How does it feel to be a winner?" she asked seductively, smiling before kissing him.

"I have a wife!" Andrew protested, pushing her away.

She licked her upper lip, laughed, and asked, "What do you need her for? Does she have this?" She moved in a slow, seductive dance, her body swaying gracefully.

"I..." Andrew began, but she interrupted him.

"Shhh..." she said, covering his mouth with her finger. "You don't even love Sarah..."

Andrew's eyes widened in surprise. How did she know his wife's name? Maybe he had mentioned it on TV and she was just a devoted fan.

He turned her against the wall and continued to kiss her passionately.

"ANDREW..." a hoarse voice echoed in the bathroom.

Andrew opened his eyes to see the girl's face had transformed into that of a rotting, smiling corpse. Her once beautiful features were now decomposed, with sunken eyes, exposed teeth through decaying lips, and skin that hung in putrid patches. The stench of death wafted into his nostrils, causing him to gag. He recoiled in horror, rubbing his lips in disgust, trying to erase the memory of her touch. In the next moment, her face returned to its beautiful form. Trembling, Andrew stumbled out of the bathroom, leaving her laughing flirtatiously behind.

"There you are! Congratulations!" the producer greeted him, holding a Grammy.

"Has the ceremony already taken place?" Andrew asked, confused.

"What are you under?" the producer laughed.

"You gave a speech, accepted the Grammy, handed it to me, and went to the bathroom," the producer explained quickly.

"Um..." Andrew mumbled.

"Here you go, show your wife," the producer said, handing him the award. "Can you drive?"

"Yes..." Andrew replied, trying to piece together what had happened.

Mr. Belfort led Andrew to his car.

"Knock knock," the producer tapped on the window.

"Huh?" Andrew said, not recognizing who was knocking. He looked around, dazed.

"Andrew!" the voice came again.

Seeing Bradley Belfort, Andrew rubbed his eyes and opened the window, yawning.

"You fell asleep just getting behind the wheel. Let me give you a ride," the producer suggested.

Andrew waved him off and began searching for something in the car compartment. His vision blurred, and his hands trembled as he fumbled through the glove box. Finally, he found a small bottle with a substance and a tiny spoon inside.

"This will wake me up," he muttered, scratching the powder out with the spoon.

"You're funny..." the producer chuckled.

Andrew inhaled the contents three times. The world around him brightened, and his heart raced. His body felt warm and euphoric, the opioid coursing through his veins like liquid gold. An inexplicable surge of energy, stronger and more alive than ever.

"I'll go myself; otherwise, my wife will think I've had too much again," Andrew said, smiling vaguely.

Mr. Belfort leaned against the car door and took out an envelope. Andrew looked at him questioningly.

"Rest, you deserve it," the producer said, handing the envelope to Andrew. "Work on your relationship with your wife while you rest. Stay with your family."

Andrew, under the influence of substances, smiled, thanked him, and drove home. The sensation of the drug was like being wrapped in a warm, comforting blanket, every nerve ending tingling with a false sense of invincibility.

—m—

Sarah was frantically decorating their new house, a sanctuary she longed to make perfect. Her exhaustion from moving constantly and renting various properties had reached its peak. She craved stability, a place she could pour her love into and call home.

"Blue or green?" she muttered to herself, staring at the wallpaper samples with a furrowed brow.

"Which one does Andrew prefer? Does it even matter?" Her voice trembled with frustration. "He never comes home, never talks to the kids. It's as if we're just obstacles in his way..."

The thought left her feeling hollow. The emptiness of her days, the fear of being insignificant, of betrayal, gnawed at her.

"What have I achieved? What have I done for this family? Maybe Andrew doesn't need me anymore? He's famous now. Everyone would want to be his wife. But I was there before the fame. I believed in him when no one else did. He can't just forget that..."

Sarah folded the wallpaper samples and sank into the plush velvet sofa, her emotions overwhelming her.

"Children are growing up without a father..."

The sound of the gates slowly opening caught her attention. A dark blue car rumbled onto the property. Sarah looked out the window, bracing herself. She inhaled deeply, trying to steady her nerves, and went to greet the father of her children.

"Hi," Sarah said as she descended the grand staircase.

Her husband's entrance was anything but glamorous. His eyes were heavy-lidded, his face bloated, and his breath came in labored gasps. Sweat dotted his forehead, and his clothes hung off him disheveled. Sarah chose not to address his frequent absences and substance abuse today. She knew another argument would only deepen the chasm between them. Still, she didn't know how to confront his new habits— she couldn't accept them, but she couldn't ignore them either.

"Hi," Andrew replied wearily, stumbling slightly as he took off his shoes and collapsed onto the couch.

"How did it go?" Sarah asked, her voice carrying a mix of hope and resignation as she sat beside him.

Andrew's gaze was distant. "You would have known if you had come," he snapped, bitterness lacing his words.

Sarah felt a pang of hurt but tried to stay calm. She wanted to bridge the gap between them, to have a normal conversation for once.

"Andrew..." Sarah began, her voice calm but trembling with suppressed frustration.

"It doesn't matter," Andrew muttered, struggling to stand. "The Grammy's in the glove compartment," he pointed weakly towards the car and stumbled, barely catching himself.

Sarah's disappointment was palpable. It was impossible to ignore the glaring issues.

"Andrew, what are you missing?" she asked quietly, not wanting to alarm the children. "You have money, a wife, children, this enormous house," she gestured around their opulent home. "Is something still missing? You're not finding happiness in reality. What are you running from? I need to understand. Help me help you."

"I want to quit, I really do!" Andrew's voice grew frantic, his hands shaking. "But I can't. I stop and feel terrible, like a complete failure. I can't write, I can't think, I can't even talk. I'm nothing without it..." His voice broke.

Little Renee peeked around the corner of the second floor, clutching her plush doll with button eyes. The recent arguments had left her visibly worried. Little girl ran to her room trying to hide from yet another argument from the parents. Andrew's irritation melted as he saw her.

Andrew forced a smile, his face softening. But Sarah's frustration was unrelenting.

"You succeeded without these substances. You were clean, you were present for us. Are we nothing to you? Why are you abandoning what you had before all this?" Sarah's voice cracked, tears welling up in her eyes.

"That's not what I mean…" Andrew said, closing his eyes in frustration. "I just feel awful without it. My body, my mind… they rebel. I feel lost."

Sarah moved closer, kneeling on the floor and taking his hands in hers. Her gaze was earnest, filled with hope and desperation.

"How would you feel if I started using these things?" she asked, searching for a solution, looking into Andrew's eyes with a mixture of sadness and hope.

Andrew thought about it. On one hand, it seemed like an escape from endless arguments and moral lectures. Maybe their love could become stronger, more connected, if they shared these indulgences. The thought of a life without endless strife, where they could experience a constant high together, almost tempted him.

Yet, he considered their children. What kind of life would they have if both parents were constantly under the influence? What if they both died from an overdose? Who would take care of the kids? No, Andrew couldn't bear the thought of his children ending up in an orphanage. It was his dream to give them a stable family.

"I… I agree," Andrew managed to say, pulling an envelope from his jacket pocket and handing it to Sarah.

"Maybe a change of scenery will help. I'll try…" he said, his voice soft.

Sarah opened the envelope and found four cruise ship tickets. Her eyes sparkled with a flicker of hope.

"Are you suggesting a vacation?" she asked, her voice barely containing her excitement.

After so much time apart, Sarah craved this chance. She waited eagerly for his confirmation.

"We'll go as a family," Andrew said, offering a genuine smile.

Sarah's face lit up with joy.

"Can you help me decide on the wallpaper for the bedroom?" she asked.

"Of course..." Andrew said tenderly, brushing Sarah's hair behind her ear and kissing her forehead.

With his arm around her, they climbed the grand staircase together, heading towards the second floor and a glimpse of a possible new beginning.

—⁂—

"Mr. Belfort, here's your coffee!" Lilith purred as she glided into the office, her smile a blend of charm and calculation.

Bradley Belfort, standing next to his shelf of accolades, proudly examined the gleaming replica of Andrew's Grammy. Though the real award was with Andrew, this replica served as a symbol of Bradley's inflated sense of self-importance.

"Thank you, dear," Bradley said, his voice laced with satisfaction as he carefully placed the replica on the shelf, positioning it just so. "What's on the agenda today?"

"Your schedule is clear," Lilith replied, her smile widening, hinting at her deeper, more dangerous motives.

Bradley's eyes lit up with a predatory glint. "Andrew's doing great. I'm quite pleased with how things are shaping up," he said, subtly patting his pocket, which was filled with the rewards of his manipulations.

Lilith's smile grew even more enigmatic. "I'll take care of him," she said, her voice a seductive whisper as she exited the room, leaving behind an air of unresolved tension.

Settling into his luxurious leather chair—a throne fit for his self-styled royalty—Bradley took a slow, deliberate drag from his expensive cigar. The rich smoke curled around him as he leaned back, savoring the opulence of his surroundings.

Dring, Dring!!!

The sharp ring of the phone shattered the silence, making Bradley's heart race with anticipation. He grabbed the receiver with a practiced hand.

"Hello?"

"Bradley Belfort? This is Oliver Hughes. I have an offer for over forty million euros."

Bradley's face lit up with a greedy, almost predatory smile. "I'm listening."

"We're ready to book Andrew Brown and Matthew Miller for a two-week tour of Europe," Oliver's voice crackled, rich with promise.

"Perfect," Bradley said, barely containing his excitement. "I'll contact them and get back to you. Goodbye."

"Thank you! See you soon," Oliver said before hanging up.

Bradley hung up the phone, his grin widening as he dialed Andrew's number. Suddenly, a chilling presence seemed to fill the room.

"Hooray for fate! Another miracle, Mr. Belfort," a middle-aged man said, his voice dripping with sarcasm.

Bradley turned, startled. "Ah, Devil. What brings you here?" he asked, his nervous laughter revealing a crack in his composure.

The Devil, standing by the window, was a dark silhouette against the dim light filtering in. His presence seemed to warp the surrounding air, casting long, eerie shadows that twisted unnaturally. His eyes, glowing with a sinister light, pierced through the gloom.

"Your greed is as formidable as it is blind," the Devil said, his voice an icy whisper that seemed to seep into Bradley's bones.

Bradley's face paled as a shiver of dread ran down his spine. "Oh, come on, it's a good day. Look at Andrew. He's got a Grammy now!"

The Devil's lips curled into a malevolent grin, revealing sharp, predatory teeth that glinted in the dim light. "Did he? All by himself?" He laced his voice with mockery and bore into Bradley with a gaze full of malevolence that seemed to darken the very air.

Bradley's heart pounded as the room seemed to close in around him. The walls appeared to constrict; the air growing thick and suffocating. He gripped the armrests of his chair, trying to steady himself, but the sense of impending doom was overwhelming.

As the Devil stepped closer, his shadow twisted grotesquely, as if it had a life of its own. The temperature in the room plummeted, and Bradley could see his breath fogging in the icy air. The Devil's presence seemed to chill him to the core.

"You're so adept at this, Bradley," the Devil said, his voice a chilling rasp. "Keep up the good work. Your destiny awaits."

As the Devil's words echoed with a haunting finality, Bradley felt a wave of sheer terror. He struggled to breathe, his mind racing as the oppressive darkness of the room threatened to engulf him. All that the great Mr. Belfort could do is to listen closely as a lost child to what the King of Hell had to say.

—ɯ—

In their lavishly decorated bedroom, with its opulent velvet drapes and polished mahogany furniture, Andrew and Sarah lay intertwined under the soft glow of an antique bedside lamp. The room exuded a sense of refined luxury, from the plush Persian rug underfoot to the golden accents that adorned the walls.

"I was just thinking about how you helped me with chemistry," Sarah said, her voice light with laughter as she nestled against Andrew's chest. Her fingers traced idle patterns on his skin, seeking the warmth of the connection.

Andrew smiled, his hand gently caressing her back. "Really? What brought that up?"

Sarah's laughter was a soft, melodious sound that filled the room, a stark contrast to the turmoil she felt inside. She wrapped herself around him, seeking comfort in the intimacy they once had. In this moment, it felt like everything might be perfect, if only for a fleeting second.

"I…" Andrew started, but his voice faltered as he tried to find the right words.

Just then, the sound of small feet pattering across the floor interrupted their tender moment. Noah burst into the room, clutching a photograph tightly. "Dad? Who is this?"

Andrew sat up abruptly, his heart sinking as he recognized the image of Grace, the very picture he had hoped would remain unseen.

"Grace? Why do you have her picture?" Sarah asked, puzzled and a bit alarmed.

"This is Mom's friend," Andrew quickly explained to Noah.

"And where did you find it?" Sarah asked, her curiosity piqued.

"In Dad's jacket," Noah replied innocently.

Sarah's emotions were a tangled mess. On one hand, she was finally sharing a peaceful moment with Andrew, yet on the other, she couldn't understand why he had Grace's photo in his jacket. It stirred something unsettling within her.

"Why do you need her picture?" Sarah asked, her voice tense.

Andrew's face showed discomfort, his lips pursed as he struggled to find the right words.

"I've been feeling pretty lost lately..." he admitted, his tone weary.

Sarah listened with a patience born from deep concern.

"During prom, we talked about my father and..." Andrew trailed off.

"Explain..." Sarah urged, her voice steady but strained.

Andrew scratched his head, a sheen of sweat forming on his brow.

"Grace told me she was an orphan too. It helps me remember there are others who have had it just as tough, especially when I think about my father..."

Sarah's heart tightened. She could barely contain her shock and hurt. Tears welled up in her eyes.

"She said that..." Sarah said, her voice breaking.

Noah, sensing his mother's distress, began to cry as well.

"Mom?" he asked through his tears.

"It's okay, Noah..." Andrew tried to soothe his son, wiping away the boy's tears. "What's wrong?" he asked Sarah gently.

Sarah moved away from Andrew's touch, her pain evident.

"Why do you need her picture?" she asked again, her voice tinged with desperation.

Andrew sighed, his eyes dropping to the floor.

"I don't know... I... When I started making headlines, I thought my father might reach out. But he hasn't. Grace's picture... it's like a reminder of a time when I didn't have to question everything about my past."

"So, Grace, someone who almost drove us apart, now becomes your anchor?" Sarah asked, her tears flowing freely.

"She's an orphan! Her parents are gone, just like mine could be. Her picture helps me remember a time when I wasn't obsessed with what my father did or didn't do," Andrew explained, his voice rising with frustration.

Before Sarah could respond, Andrew's phone rang. He glanced at the caller ID. "Mr. Belfort."

"Damn it. I've got to take this. Bradley's calling..." Andrew said, grabbing his bathrobe.

Sarah watched as her husband left the room. She gently placed Noah down and wiped her own tears, trying to regain her composure.

Downstairs, Andrew answered the call, his attention shifting to the conversation with the producer.

"Hello?"

"Andrew!" Bradley's voice brimmed with excitement as he announced, "We have been offered $40 million euros for a two-week European tour!"

Andrew's eyes widened with a mix of awe and desire.

"Forty million... Can I talk to Sarah first?" he asked, his voice betraying his eagerness.

"No time. The tour starts tomorrow. Afterward, you can enjoy your riches with your family for the rest of your life," Bradley said.

"Alright. What time should we be there?"

"9 am sharp. The plane will be ready."

"Got it."

Andrew turned back towards the bedroom, but Sarah and Noah were no longer there. He went to the kitchen, where he found Sarah comforting their son.

"Sarah..." Andrew said softly, approaching her. "I love you. I shouldn't hide things from you..."

Sarah looked up, her eyes red from crying.

"Say something," Andrew prompted.

"All right. Just... explain to me why Grace's picture matters so much to you," Sarah said, her voice strained but determined.

Andrew took a deep breath.

"It's not just about her. It's about how she made me feel understood. I thought maybe she had some answers, or at least shared some of the same pain."

Sarah kissed Noah's forehead as he settled down.

"When Grace first came to live with me, I made sure she felt like family. I told my parents to spend time with her, and treated her like a sister. But she still felt rejected. She told you she was an orphan. That's not the whole truth, and it hurts that she misled you like that."

Andrew walked over and wrapped his arms around Sarah.

"I didn't know, Sarah. I'm sorry. Come here..."

They moved into a slow, comforting dance. Andrew held Sarah close, his hands finding their way to her delicate frame. Sarah rested her head on his shoulder, her breath mingling with his. The room was quiet, save for the soft strains of music from a nearby speaker.

"Why are we dancing?" Sarah asked, a small smile forming as she followed his lead.

"Just... wanted to hold you, remind you that we're in this together," Andrew said softly, his eyes meeting hers with genuine affection.

Their connection, though strained, was a lifeline in the storm of their emotions. As they swayed together, the luxurious details of their life seemed to dissolve, leaving only the warmth of their shared affection.

In this quiet, intimate moment, they found solace in each other. Despite their imperfections, their love remained a steady flame. Andrew's touch was gentle, and as he spun Sarah around, they both felt a renewed sense of closeness and understanding. The world outside seemed to vanish, leaving them in a cocoon of warmth and tenderness.

Andrew walked down the dimly lit corridor, each step echoing through the darkness. As he advanced, the light seemed to recede, enveloping him in a deepening gloom. The shadows thickened until the hallway was a suffocating black void. He came to a halt, paralyzed by the encroaching darkness.

"Andrew..." a rasping, almost inhuman voice called out from the abyss.

He stood frozen, his heart hammering, his hands clenched into tight fists. The silence was almost deafening. Suddenly, a door creaked open, bathing the corridor in a harsh, blinding light. Andrew squinted, his nerves on edge, and stepped through the doorway.

He found himself in a child's room, cluttered with bright, cheerful drawings and scattered toys. Among them was a blue sports car, a miniature version of Andrew's own vehicle. As he picked up the toy, the memories of his childhood began to flood back.

"Andrew," his mother's voice echoed gently from another room.

The voice was a haunting reminder of a time long past. Andrew moved hesitantly towards the source of the sound, opening the next door to reveal his parents' bedroom. The room seemed to pulse with the echoes of old fights: the sharp clang of broken dishes, the angry shouts, the stinging silence of cold confrontations. Andrew's shoulders slumped as the weight of those memories engulfed him.

A younger version of himself, clutching the blue car, appeared in his mind. "When I grow up, I will never hurt my family," the child vowed earnestly.

Andrew watched as his younger self played with the toy car.

"I definitely won't drink," the boy continued, his voice filled with innocent conviction. "I'll try, but I won't drink much!"

Andrew managed a sad smile, but it slowly faded as the boy's next words struck him with a harsh reality.

"And I won't take drugs," the child declared with naïve certainty.

"I definitely won't be like you!" the boy yelled, throwing the car toward Andrew with a burst of anger.

Andrew ducked as the toy skidded across the floor. When he looked back, the boy was gone. Desperately, he searched the room for any sign of the child, but it was as if he had vanished into thin air.

"Andrew..." The same hoarse voice called again, this time from the bathroom.

Fury and dread surged through him. "Father..." He opened the bathroom door with a trembling hand, only to find the room empty. His gaze fell upon the mirror, and his blood ran cold.

In the reflection, his face twisted grotesquely. The image before him was not his own but a nightmarish creature: hollow, dark sockets where eyes should have been, an animalistic grin stretched wide, revealing jagged, sharp teeth. The face was a cruel mockery of his own, radiating an overwhelming, sinister malevolence.

"Andrew!!!" The voice roared from the depths of the mirror, a guttural scream that seemed to shake the very foundation of his sanity.

Andrew staggered back, overwhelmed by a searing pain in his head. His legs felt weak, and he slumped against the sink, struggling to overcome the cacophony of terror that assailed him. His reflection loomed menacingly, a distorted, monstrous version of himself.

Morning. 8:30.

Andrew jolted awake, drenched in sweat, his heart racing. He scrambled to dress, his mind still reeling from the nightmare.

"Damn it!" he muttered, throwing on clothes hastily.

Sarah stirred, her eyes fluttering open.

"Where are you going?" she asked, her voice laced with concern.

Andrew turned to face her, trying to mask his anxiety.

"Would you choose forty million euros or a luxury cruise?" he asked, attempting to sound casual.

Sarah's eyes widened, her sleepiness evaporating into alarm.

"What's happening? Did Bradley make you an offer? Do you know what I've told the kids?" Her tone was sharp, filled with worry.

Andrew took a deep breath, laying out the situation.

"A two-week tour in Europe. Forty million euros. We could secure our future, live in luxury, buy amazing gifts for everyone!" he said, trying to paint it as an opportunity.

"Are we in financial trouble? Are we going back to struggling?" Sarah's voice wavered.

"No, it's not that..." Andrew began, but Sarah cut him off.

"Then why? We already have everything we need. Why do you want more money?" Her frustration grew, tears welling in her eyes.

"You don't understand! Even if life is good now, this is a rare chance to secure our future. Forty million euros is a fortune!" he said, his hands gesturing wildly.

"Stay with your family! The kids barely see you. I hardly see you. Does our time together mean so little?" Sarah's voice broke, tears spilling freely.

"It's not like that. I have to go. You'll understand later..." Andrew said, pulling on his jacket and heading for the door.

Downstairs, Noah looked up at his father with tearful eyes.

"Did Mommy upset you? Aren't we going on vacation?" he asked, his voice trembling.

Andrew crouched down, smoothing Noah's hair.

"I love your mom. It's okay. We're not going on vacation, but I promise I'll get you a really cool toy, okay?" he said, trying to soothe him.

Noah nodded reluctantly, his sadness still evident. Andrew went out the door, leaving behind a heartbroken Sarah and a confused child.

—◆—

Already ten minutes late, Andrew sped along the highway, overtaking cars with reckless urgency. The panic from his nightmare still clung to him like a second skin. His mind raced with thoughts of Sarah and the children, their faces haunting him. As he approached the airport gate, he fumbled in the glove compartment for his pills, swallowing several at once without counting.

"Mr. Brown!" the border guard greeted the artist. "You are expected."

Andrew drove on, entering the hangar. He hurriedly got out of the car and ran to the plane where his producer was waiting.

"Sorry I'm late. It took a while to explain things to Sarah," Andrew said, breathless.

Mr. Belfort, the producer, greeted him with open arms. "A personal plane doesn't leave without its main passenger," he said, handing more pills to the staggering Andrew.

"I've already taken a few," Andrew responded, his expression dazed.

"How many?" Belfort asked, chuckling.

"I don't know, two or three," Andrew replied.

"Here, have two more. It's a long flight," the producer insisted.

Andrew swallowed the pills with a vague smile, his head tilting back in a moment of inertia.

"Come on, Matthew's already inside," Bradley said, ushering Andrew onto the plane.

Andrew greeted Matthew, staggering slightly, and found a seat.

"Welcome aboard!" a pretty stewardess smiled at them.

Champagne exploded, girls danced, and Lilith, impeccable as always, was there as Bradley's assistant. After several toasts no one could remember, and a few songs, the effects of the pills began to wear off. Eyes began to close with exhaustion. Bradley was the first to fall asleep. Andrew and Matthew, however, were deep in conversation.

"A year ago, we wouldn't have sat like this," Matthew marveled, gesturing around the private plane. "Thousands of meters in the sky, behind a bar, in a private plane." He laughed at their past.

Andrew, leaning against the counter, closed his eyes and smiled. "Yes…"

"We did it, man!" Matthew raised his glass.

"We?" Andrew thought bitterly. His eyes opened, and he straightened up. "Did you sell your soul to the devil too?" he asked, grinning.

"What are you talking about?" Matthew replied, confused.

Andrew laughed, a harsh, unnatural sound. "What did you personally do?" he asked, his eyes piercing into Matthew's.

Matthew frowned, struggling to process Andrew's words through his intoxication. "What did I do? What does the Devil have to do with it?"

"Do you believe in God?" Andrew asked, his voice losing its fear.

"I don't know… Probably yes…" Matthew said uncertainly.

Andrew moved closer. "Do you believe in the Devil?"

Matthew laughed nervously. "He won't remember… I won't even remember," Andrew muttered to himself. "If you believe in God, then you believe in the Devil," he said, raising his voice.

Matthew tensed at Andrew's behavior. Andrew made a grand gesture with his hand. "Look! The devil!" he said mockingly. "Please! Give me phenomenal success on the tour and a bottle of good gin in the fridge!"

Matthew, watching the scene, laughed a little. Andrew reached into the refrigerator and pulled out a premium gin bottle. "Impossible! Think about it… We're in a private jet, of course the fridge is stocked!" Matthew said, trying to rationalize it.

Andrew drank from the bottle, grinning. Matthew, to prove his point, got up and opened the fridge. He froze. "There was only one bottle of gin… everything else was whiskey and wine…"

Andrew laughed harder. "I'm a drug addict and an alcoholic… the children don't know if I love them, Sarah is in tears every morning…" he said sadly, looking down. "But the plane!" he said sarcastically, spreading his arms wide.

Matthew sat back down, contemplating. "So, the devil, God, and angels are all true?" he asked, frightened.

"Yes," Andrew replied shortly.

Matthew closed his eyes and fell asleep in his comfortable seat.

"Hello, Mr. Brown," a voice came from Matthew's place.

Andrew turned to see a middle-aged man. "You've achieved a lot since our last meeting… How do you like the bottle of gin?" The Devil poured a glass and pushed it toward Andrew.

Andrew, pointing at his sleeping friend, said, "Free will, huh?"

"Did I force drinks and pills down his throat?" the Devil retorted, pushing the glass.

Andrew laughed, took the glass, and emptied it. "An old, homeless man, on the day we met… Is that my father?" he asked.

"Do you really want to know the truth?" the Devil replied.

"No…" Andrew said after a moment.

"What's bothering you?" the Devil asked calmly.

Andrew tapped his empty glass, looking at Matthew. "Your friend… when was the last time you met as friends? How's the family?" the Devil continued.

Andrew twisted the glass in his hand. "Of course… Only because of you, they have achieved success. At the expense of your talents. Without you, they would not have flown to perform a phenomenal performance…" the Devil said.

"I had a dream today… there was something in the mirror. It's not like my dream… who was in the mirror?" Andrew asked, changing the subject.

"Of all the things you can ask, you're asking me to decipher your dreams?" the Devil replied, smiling.

Andrew, irritated by the constant questions instead of answers, asked, "What do I need to ask?"

The Devil grinned and took an envelope from his pocket, showing it to Andrew.

"What is it?" Andrew asked.

"Why don't you decide for yourself?" the Devil said, putting the envelope on the counter.

"Who was that in the mirror?" Andrew repeated.

"Andrew…" the Devil said, his voice blending with Lilith's.

"Boarding in 10 minutes, will you sit in your chair?" Lilith's voice called.

Andrew looked at the empty place where the Devil had been, then back at Lilith. She raised her eyebrows, waiting for him to move.

"Yeah," Andrew replied, picking up the envelope and following her to his chair.

—⚶—

Dublin, London, Paris, Milan, Rome, Monaco, Barcelona, Madrid, Lisbon, Berlin, Copenhagen, Vienna—tour after tour, performance after performance. Autographs, paparazzi, and crowds of screaming fans addicted to Andrew and Matthew's songs.

Andrew stood on stage, shouting back at the sea of thousands. The energy was electrifying. Stomping, clapping, shouting, flashes, lights, music, drums—and in the middle of it all, Andrew, the man elevated above everyone, raised his hands in triumph, feeding off the adoration of the crowd.

"I…" Andrew began, panting from the exertion of the concert, "I want to… I want to say that…"

"Andrew Brown!" Matthew interrupted, stepping forward.

The crowd erupted in deafening cheers. Matthew gently took the microphone from Andrew.

"I think you've had enough performances for today," Matthew whispered into Andrew's ear.

Andrew locked eyes with Matthew, his breath coming in heavy gasps. His eyes were glassy, his mouth hung open, and sweat glistened on his forehead.

"I'm thirsty..." Andrew managed to say, his voice strained.

Matthew pointed towards the backstage area with a smile. Andrew swayed, struggling to keep his balance.

"Andrew, get off the stage, you're not in any state to say anything," Matthew said firmly.

With wobbly legs, Andrew stumbled off the stage and into the backstage area.

"We thank all our listeners..." Matthew began addressing the audience.

Reaching the end of the stage, Andrew's legs gave out entirely. He collapsed, his dry tongue protruding as he licked his sweaty lips for moisture.

"Phenomenal performance, keep it up!" the producer praised.

"Yeah," Andrew replied cynically, grabbing a glass of gin and ice from the piano.

He drank greedily, tilting his head back further and further, as if the gin were the elixir of life.

"Andrew... your wife is calling you," Lilith smiled coquettishly, stepping closer.

"ANDREW..." a hoarse voice echoed in his ears as he finished the glass and collapsed to the ground.

Lilith laughed and sat down beside him, gently wiping sweat and gin from his cheek. "Sarah asks when you're coming," she said, handing the phone to Andrew.

"My love! How are you?" Andrew greeted his wife, laughing into the phone.

"Andrew? Are you okay?" Sarah asked, her voice filled with worry.

"Mmm..." Andrew mumbled, lighting a cigarette.

As Sarah spoke, Lilith took the cigarette from Andrew, inhaled, smiled, and placed it back on his lips.

"You know, I called you, and a girl, Lilith, picked up the phone, said you were busy... What are you doing?! Have you been busy with her these two months?!"

"No, I'm at the concert..."

"Are you at the concert?! Why the hell am I waiting for you with the kids at the airport?!"

"Damn... I'm sorry... I forgot to tell you about the concert today..."

"How many more concerts will you have? Who are you doing this for? Two months have already passed!"

"I will come in a week, I promise..."

Sarah hung up. Andrew's relaxed face twisted into a hateful grin. He rolled over and smashed the phone on the floor.

Back on the tour bus, Andrew and Matthew sat in tense silence, the roar of the road filling the void. Andrew's hand shook slightly as he poured another drink.

"Do you think you can keep this up?" Matthew asked, his tone edged with concern and frustration.

Andrew didn't meet his gaze. "What's that supposed to mean?"

"Look at yourself, man. You're falling apart. Sarah's at her wit's end, the kids hardly see you…"

Andrew downed the drink and stared at the empty glass. "This is what we signed up for. Fame, money… isn't this what we wanted?"

Matthew leaned forward, his voice lowering. "At what cost, Andrew? You're destroying everything around you. Your family, your health… It's not worth it."

Andrew's eyes flicked to Matthew, a dangerous glint in them. "Don't lecture me. You're enjoying the ride too."

"But I'm not the one spiraling out of control. You need help, Andrew."

Andrew laughed bitterly. "Help? From who? You? The guy who's riding my coattails?"

Matthew's expression hardened. "You're not the only one who's worked for this. Don't act like you're alone in this."

Andrew's laughter died in his throat, replaced by a stony stare. "Maybe I am."

The bus hit a bump, and the jolt seemed to snap something inside Andrew. He stood abruptly, swaying slightly. "I need air." Signaling the bus driver to stop, Andrew got out of the vehicle.

Outside, the chilly night air hit Andrew like a slap. He leaned against the bus, the world spinning. He pulled out his phone, his hand shaking as he dialed his wife.

"Hello, Andrew," the Devil's voice was smooth, like silk over steel.

Andrew's heart pounded. "Why did you show up?"

"Why are you so bitter? You're getting everything you wanted, aren't you?"

Andrew looked at his reflection in the bus window, seeing a hollow, haunted man. "This... this isn't what I wanted."

"Isn't it? Fame, fortune, adoration... you asked, and I delivered."

"But I'm losing everything that matters," Andrew whispered, the weight of his choices crushing him.

The Devil's laugh was soft, almost pitiful. "You made your bed, Andrew. Now lie in it. Enjoy the fruits of your labor. If you truly desired peace and a happy family life, you'd have that long ago..."

"Who are you talking to?" Mathew asked his colleague, looking from the bus window.

"Nobody..." a bit startled by the sudden disappearance of the Devil.

"Done taking air? We need to move"

Andrew nodded in understanding, staring at his reflection, his own hollow eyes staring back.

—⟡—

The small room, filled with the scent of incense and the soft glow of candles, was a sanctuary of secrets. Shyla, known to her clients as Madame Faith, was finishing up a session with a regular customer.

"I am your frequent customer… Can you make a discount please?" asked the client.

After a moment of consideration, Shyla smiled and spread her arms. "Of course! Forty-five hundred, ten percent."

Reluctantly, the man took out his wallet from his custom-made jacket and handed her the bills. "Thank you," he said, bowing slightly as he left the room.

"Great…" Shyla muttered to herself, opening her notebook. "Laura, 3:30…" she read, preparing for her next session.

A middle-aged man, unknown to Shyla, entered the room. His presence was unsettling, a dark energy following him as he approached her desk.

"Good afternoon," the stranger said calmly, his voice carrying an unnerving resonance.

"Hello, did you make an appointment?" Shyla asked with a polite smile, masking her unease.

The man began to explore the various mysterious objects in Shyla's room, his movements deliberate and almost predatory. "No," he replied, his attention focused on an Egyptian sculpture.

"A client will come in 10 minutes. Let me sign you up for next week," Shyla said, reaching for her appointment book.

The man turned to her, his eyes boring into hers. "Don't worry, Mia, I won't be long."

Shyla's heart skipped a beat. "Who are you?" she asked, her voice quivering.

The man grinned and sat down at her table. "Don't you know yourself? You have a gift..." he said sarcastically, raising his hands in a mockery of a sorcerer's gesture.

Fear gripped Shyla's heart. "How do you know my name?" she demanded, her voice shaky.

The stranger laughed, a sound that sent chills down her spine. "Are you trying to use your gift?" he taunted.

"I don't know who you are... what do you want? Money? Have you come to expose me?" Shyla's voice rose in panic.

"Sarah Brown, and the shadow behind her husband's back... You wanted to talk to her, right?" The Devil's eyes seemed to pierce her soul. "Why don't you find out for yourself?"

The thirst for knowledge enveloped Shyla. She reached for her tarot cards, her hands trembling. As she shuffled them, the first card fell out: the "Two of Swords."

"Uncertainty before a choice, deep thoughts... You will have ... or you had a difficult choice, you presented several options for the development of the event ..." she said, placing the card in the center of the table.

Continuing to shuffle, the second card fell out: "King of Swords."

"A domineering man, mercantile. Are you a lawyer?" she suggested.

"Partially," the man replied, his eyes never leaving the cards.

The third card: "Magician."

"The illusionist..." Shyla mused aloud. "Broker?"

The stranger remained silent, his gaze fixed on her with an intensity that made her skin crawl. A card fell face down from the deck. She began to put it back, but he stopped her.

"The laws of attraction sometimes make it difficult to understand the whole picture," he hinted, his voice a sinister whisper.

Shyla hesitated, then examined the fourth card: "The Moon."

"You are a big entrepreneur..." she ventured.

"I have a sin there," the Devil remarked playfully.

Pulling out the fifth card: "The Hanged Man."

"You are an arms dealer..." Shyla revealed, her voice barely a whisper.

The man grinned, a chilling sight. "The cards don't lie, maybe I'm interpreting them inaccurately, but it's you," she insisted, moving closer.

"I'm not lying either," he said slowly. "Let's look at the last card."

As she shuffled, two cards fell out. One read: "Death." Shyla pushed the card towards the spread and reached for the inverted card.

"Laura won't come to you anymore. There was a sharp stabbing pain in her heart this morning. An urgent operation is being performed on her now, but alas, she will not survive," the Devil said, his tone eerily calm.

Shyla's hand froze. The seventh card: "The Devil."

Her heart pounded in her chest, her skin prickling with goosebumps. The room seemed to grow colder, her breath visible in the sudden chill. She glanced at the spread, and all six cards read "Devil."

"Nice to meet you," the stranger smiled, a wicked glint in his eyes.

"You… Are you the Devil?" Shyla's voice was a mere whisper, trembling with fear. "Did Laura really die in surgery?"

"She will die," he answered, his tone devoid of emotion.

Hesitantly, Shyla began to gather the cards, her mind racing. "Does it mean that hell, heaven, God, demons are all true?" she asked, her voice barely audible.

The Devil nodded slowly, his gaze never wavering. "Are you that shadow?" Shyla asked, her voice shaking.

"I am its conductor," he replied, his eyes piercing into her soul.

Shyla looked at her watch: 3:32. The Devil did not lie. "What do you want most of all? Money? Power?" she asked through gritted teeth.

"But you're the Devil… We can't negotiate with you," Shyla said, trying to muster courage.

"Who can I talk to?" The man interrupted her. "With God?" The Devil's sarcasm was palpable.

Shyla opened her mouth to respond but found herself speechless. If she said yes, she would contradict the lord of death himself. If she said no, she would sell her soul to the Devil.

"Why do you people consider me to be the opposite of God? After all, I am the most famous humanist in the history of mankind. I am the most generous! A person desires something, asks God, and hopes for the fulfillment of his desires. And I provide everything!" the stranger gesticulated wildly.

"Because of you, people go to hell," Shyla accused.

"Because of me?" the Devil asked again. "Aren't you the ones who accept bribes, borrow money, elevate, feed your beloved ego?"

"Aren't you the ones who torture souls in hell? Isn't it because of you that there are wars and diseases in the world?" Shyla challenged him.

The Devil leaned back and laughed, a sound that echoed through the room like the wail of lost souls. "First of all, you people torture yourself with regrets, expectations, and fears..." he paused, his eyes narrowing. "Secondly, how do you know if you're in hell or not? What can you people talk about with confidence?"

"I know I'm alive. I remember what happened yesterday, I have plans for tomorrow, I feel like I'm here and now," Shyla explained, her voice shaking.

"Aha!" the stranger exclaimed, leaping from his chair. "What if I told you that you are living an endless loop, repeating over and over, over and over again? What if I told you that this is not the first time I've had this conversation with you, or even the thousandth time? What if the loop repeats itself in a certain case, such as death?" The Devil's words were rapid, his tone maddeningly cheerful.

"The Bible and all the scriptures say not to believe you! For you are the tempter!" Shyla cried, remembering God.

"Am I the tempter?!" The Devil shouted triumphantly, a sudden flash of lightning illuminating his face in a ghastly blue. "I am the ruler of this world!" His voice thundered, the room trembling as the electricity cut out. "I am the lord Satan! Recognize your prince and you will live a life you never dreamed of! Do you want knowledge?" The Devil's eyes gleamed with a terrifying intensity.

"Stop it! Please! My lord! I have sinned... I desired knowledge forbidden to man, and received the gift of visions, and used it for selfish purposes!" Shyla fell to her knees, tears streaming down her face.

The man stopped, a devilish smile spreading across his face. "I am not God, and I am not all-merciful. I give you all the forbidden knowledge. From now on, I am your lord, and you will answer for your sins." His voice multiplied, echoing in Shyla's ears. "With the permission of my father's Lord, I will cast you alive into the lake of fire and brimstone, where you will suffer day and night forever and ever." His words resounded like a death knell.

Shyla began to pray, whispering a desperate plea to God. The Devil watched with twisted delight. "You don't know yourself, how do you know God?" he mocked.

Drawing a cross in the air with his right hand, the Devil intoned, "In the name of the father and the son and the Holy Spirit, I bless you for God's forgiveness."

Shyla felt a brief, deceptive moment of relief, her body relaxing. But then the Devil continued, "In the name of me, the beast and the false prophet, I punish you for your sins." He drew an inverted cross with his left hand, his pleasure palpable.

Pointing his index finger at Shyla, the Devil's face contorted with euphoria. As he laughed maniacally, Shyla's health deteriorated rapidly. Her vision darkened, her body weakened, and her heartbeat slowed. The coldness enveloped her, and darkness turned to complete gloom. Amidst the Devil's laughter, she aged to the appearance of a mummy in a few moments.

A sleek black car glided up to the gate of Andrew's house. Inside, Andrew, slouched in the backseat, finished the last swig from a bottle of gin.

"Damn... do we have more?" he asked, pushing his greasy hair back.

"No, sorry boss," the driver replied, his voice tinged with guilt.

Andrew leaned back, his gaze fixed on the roof of the car. He replayed the day's events in his mind: a potential quarrel with his wife, the hollow promises of shorter tours, the tears of his children. The thought of returning to that tumult was almost unbearable. He closed his eyes, trying to drown out the noise of his own thoughts with the echoes of his audience—cheers, applause, the roar of the crowd. Breathing deeply, he tried to relax, his body swaying to an imagined rhythm. He began to tap his fingers, mimicking the beat of his song.

"Are you okay?" the driver asked, glancing at Andrew through the rearview mirror.

"Yeah..." Andrew replied with a slight cough, his eyes still closed.

He gathered himself, slid on his sunglasses, and opened the door.

"Is that an acquaintance of yours?" the driver asked, pointing to a figure standing near the gate.

Andrew's gaze shifted to the figure and recognized his father. A wave of mixed emotions—resentment, pity, love—washed over him.

"Yeah... good night," Andrew said, stepping out of the car.

Approaching the old man, Andrew's thoughts churned. What did he really feel for him? Anger? Compassion? Disgust?

"Andrew?" the old man called out softly.

Andrew approached with a cold demeanor.

"Take off your glasses, please. It's night outside," the old man said, his voice tinged with a faint plea.

Andrew removed his sunglasses, revealing bloodshot eyes. The old man's gaze was both assessing and regretful.

"Look at you... Aren't you sick of yourself? Your eyes are swollen, you can barely breathe, your hair is dirty..."

167

"Do you have the right to judge me?" Andrew snapped. "Where were you when I needed support? Who were you with while Mom was in tears? You're a drug addict, an alcoholic..."

"I quit a long time ago," the old man said quietly.

"Oh, did you? You left a mark on me! You quit drugs, but the damage is still here! Mom is still dead! Is that why you came? For money?" Andrew fished out crumpled hundred-dollar bills and threw them at his father.

"I'm sorry your image of me is shattered. Do you want the same for your children?" the old man said, his voice heavy with sadness.

"My children?! Get out of here! Don't come back! I hate you!" Andrew shouted, a twisted grin on his face.

The old man lowered his head and walked away, his shoulders slumped. Andrew watched him leave, his hatred palpable. With a grunt of dissatisfaction, he put his sunglasses back on and headed for the house.

As he walked up the path, Andrew lit a cigarette, taking a slow drag. He rang the doorbell with a trembling hand. The cool night air felt refreshing against his heated skin. He balanced himself on his heels, waiting for the door to open.

"Andrew?" His wife's voice called out from inside.

Andrew snuffed out his cigarette and answered, "Yeah."

Sarah opened the door, her eyes widening at the sight of her disheveled husband.

"What's wrong with you?" she asked warily.

"I'm... just tired," Andrew replied, trying to sound nonchalant.

Sarah's gaze lingered on the package in his hand. "Have you been drinking?"

"Yeah," Andrew admitted with an indifferent shrug.

Sarah's confusion deepened as she eyed Andrew's appearance and the package. She hesitated before speaking again. "You started smoking too? Are you alright?"

Andrew collapsed onto the sofa near the entrance, a sardonic smile playing on his lips. He handed her the package, which contained various toys for the children. Sarah opened it, her expression softening slightly.

"Tomorrow night we'll fly to Italy, and from there we'll cruise by sea," Andrew said, pulling out new tickets.

"You've been gone for two months. Lilith answered your phone. You're drinking, smoking—do you think a cruise will make me forget everything?" Sarah's voice was edged with frustration.

Andrew reached for her hand, but she pulled away. "Did you cheat on me?" she demanded.

"No, she's my assistant."

"And when were you going to tell me?" Sarah asked, her voice rising.

"As soon as... Listen..." Andrew began, but Sarah cut him off.

"You listen! If you come home drunk or high again, no more excuses. I'll leave. It's been a year, Andrew. We don't feel like a family anymore. The kids even asked me at the airport if you'd be with us or working."

"Alright, alright. I get it," Andrew said, raising his hands in a placating gesture. "I'll stop. Starting today, we'll be a family."

"We'll see," Sarah replied coldly. "I'm going to bed."

Without another word, she turned and walked toward the bedroom, leaving Andrew alone on the couch. He sank into the cushions, the weight of the evening settling heavily on him. The silence in the house was a stark contrast to the chaos of his day, a brief pause before the next chapter of his tumultuous life began.

CHAPTER

3

An old man leaned against a grimy, dark yellow wall, taking a drag from his third cigarette. His eyes darted around nervously, as if he were expecting something—or someone. The street lay dimly lit, casting long shadows that crawled over the cracked pavement like creeping phantoms.

"Shit!" a young man shouted, his voice echoing as he gestured violently at another man across the street.

The old man crushed his cigarette against the wall, leaving a smudge of ash and embers that smeared like a bruise. He moved deliberately towards the shouting man, his footsteps echoing in the quiet night like a drumbeat of impending doom.

"Hey!" the old man called out, his voice hoarse and rough, the sound of gravel being ground underfoot. "Come here!" He pointed with a trembling hand, his bony finger shaking with barely contained rage.

"What the hell are you doing here?!" the young man snarled, his eyes narrowing as he took in the old man's disheveled appearance, reeking of desperation and stale smoke.

"Where's your family? Why would you kill him? Are you high? You goddamn coward!" The old man's questions tumbled out, each word laced with venom, his voice cracking with years of pent-up anger.

"Who the hell are you to me?!" the young man snapped, shoving the old man away. "You can't even quit smoking," he added with a sneer, the acrid smell of cigarettes mingling with the tension in the air.

"I haven't had a family for a long time! And I only smoke! What about you?! Are you really that stupid?!" The old man croaked, his voice rising in pitch as he struck his own head in frustration, the impact echoing like a gavel of judgment.

"You don't have a family because you ruined it," the young man shot back, his words cutting deep, slicing through the old man's defenses.

Rage overtook the old man. With a guttural roar, he lunged at the young man, fists flying. The young man stumbled and fell to the sidewalk under the onslaught. The old man straddled him, raining down punches with unrelenting fury. Blood splattered, staining the concrete and the old man's knuckles, but he didn't stop. Time blurred as he continued to beat the young man, blow after blow, each punch a release of years of bottled-up fury and pain.

"You ruined my family," the old man finally muttered, his breath ragged as he looked down at the bloody, motionless body beneath him, his eyes wild with a mix of triumph and despair.

He fumbled in his pocket with shaking hands, pulling out a pack of cigarettes. Extracting one with bloodied fingers, he placed it in his mouth. Reaching into his back pocket, he retrieved a lighter and flicked it on. The flame sputtered but didn't catch. He tried again, and again, growing more agitated with each failed attempt. The lighter refused to work, mirroring his own impotent rage.

Cursing under his breath, he tossed the lighter into the street and rifled through the unconscious man's pockets until he found another one. Finally, he lit the cigarette and took a deep drag, savoring the harsh smoke as it burned his lungs. He stepped over the body and walked down the deserted street, the smoke curling behind him like a ghostly trail, a reminder of the violence and despair that now defined his existence.

—ɯ—

Andrew looked out the window of a cruise ship, the raging storm outside contrasting with the uneasy calm inside his cabin. Curled into a fetal position, he lay drenched in cold sweat, finding fleeting solace in isolation. His muscles ached, and he shivered uncontrollably despite the warm blankets wrapped around him. Every nerve in his body seemed to scream in agony. Twice a day, Sarah came to check on him, offering gentle support as he battled opioid withdrawal.

"I'm doing this for my family," Andrew muttered to himself, rocking back and forth. His stomach churned, and he fought the urge to vomit, a plastic bucket by his side already half-filled from earlier bouts.

"I'm proud of you," Sarah said softly, wiping his forehead with a warm cloth, her touch a small comfort in his suffering.

Days stretched into what felt like weeks as the agony of withdrawal gnawed at his resolve. Dark thoughts swirled in his mind. His skin crawled with a relentless itch, and his legs kicked involuntarily in the grip of restless leg syndrome.

"Why live like this? How will I go on without it? For the sake of the family? For what? No… It is necessary, it is better this way… I have to quit…" he murmured, his voice barely audible over the storm outside.

"And how will you write?" Bradley's mocking voice cut through his thoughts, making his heart race with anxiety.

Recognizing Bradley as a hallucination, Andrew growled, "Shut up," rolling from one side to the other. His hands trembled, and he clenched them into fists to stop the shaking.

"If you don't take it, you'll shut up yourself," Bradley taunted, his words echoing in Andrew's head like a relentless drumbeat.

Writhing in hatred for everything around him, Andrew gripped the sheets of his sweat-soaked bed, clenching his teeth. His body was wracked with cramps, and tears of frustration and pain leaked from his eyes.

"Let him be silent… We're better off without him," Mathew's voice interjected, a counterpoint to Bradley's insidious suggestions.

"What are you going to do without me?" Andrew hissed through gritted teeth, his voice barely more than a croak from the dehydration.

"There is no you," Bradley sneered, his face a twisted mask of contempt.

Barely managing to take a glass of water, Andrew hurled it at the hallucination, the glass shattering against the cabin wall, a brief release of his pent-up rage.

"You do realize that we're a part of you, right?" Mathew laughed at Andrew's fury. "And what will Sarah do without you?" he asked mockingly, his voice dripping with scorn.

Breathing heavily, Andrew's gaze darkened with hatred as he faced the hallucination. His heart pounded painfully in his chest, and his vision blurred with unshed tears.

"Sarah understands that thanks to me, she's on this cruise… because of me, you became famous," Mathew provoked, his words cutting deep.

"Fuck you… I negotiated with the producer, not you…. I sold my soul! Not you!" Andrew shouted into the empty cabin, his voice cracking.

"Andrew," a gentle voice called out, cutting through the haze of pain and confusion.

Turning, he saw Grace's apparition, her presence offering a brief respite. His lips were cracked and dry, and he licked them painfully.

"Grace," he whispered in torment, his voice hoarse.

"How are you?" she asked, wiping his forehead with a rag, her touch cool and soothing.

The hallucination faded, and Sarah reappeared, still wiping his forehead. Andrew's gaze filled with a deep sadness and regret. Heavy breathing returned, and the weight on his chest pressed down once more.

"I'm proud of you," Sarah said with tears in her eyes, kissing his forehead. "Why did you call me Grace?" she asked, her voice trembling.

"I love you," Andrew said, his voice thick with pain and emotion.

Sarah looked down, a couple of tears falling onto the sweat-soaked sheet.

"I love you too," she replied softly.

Leaving a fresh glass of water and swapping out the untouched plate of food for another, she leaned down and whispered, "Get well," before exiting the cabin, leaving Andrew alone with his torment. His muscles twitched uncontrollably, and he felt another wave of nausea rising, the struggle far from over.

—m—

Once again, Jackson fumbled with the key, struggling to fit it into the lock of his apartment door. When he finally managed to open it, Emma stood inside, her face a mixture of resignation and distress. Jackson's appearance was unmistakable: his eyes were bloodshot, his face was bloated, and a thin sheen of sweat coated his forehead.

"I'm not surprised anymore!" Emma said, her voice trembling with anger.

Jackson collapsed into a chair near the entrance, a twisted smirk spreading across his face. "My friend was at the bar..." he slurred, losing his balance and toppling to the floor. His laughter turned into a chaotic, manic cackle.

Emma hesitated, caught between the urge to help him and her growing hatred for his self-destructive behavior. She turned away, unable to bear the sight of him.

"You missed your son's birthday..." Emma said, her voice heavy with disappointment.

"Damn, is it Friday already?" Jackson's eyes widened in panic.

"It's Tuesday, Jackson... it's Tuesday," Emma corrected, her voice breaking with pain. "Why'd you even come back?"

Jackson struggled to his feet, glaring at Emma with an almost predatory intensity. "What do you think?" he snarled.

Despite the fear gnawing at her insides, Emma fought to remain calm. Thoughts of her son's well-being overwhelmed her terror. "There's no money... I paid our debts," she stated firmly.

Jackson's rage exploded. He swung his palm with brutal force, slapping Emma across the face. She crashed to the floor, her head snapping back from the impact.

"Did you spend my money?!" Jackson roared, his voice a furious bellow.

"I paid the debts!" Emma shouted back, clutching her jaw, her eyes welling with tears.

Jackson, consumed by rage, grabbed Emma by her hair and dragged her into the kitchen. "I know you're hiding it here somewhere," he growled, yanking her through the room. "Where is it?!" He began tearing open cabinets and drawers with frenzied violence, sending plates and utensils clattering to the floor.

Emma writhed in pain as Jackson threw items with reckless abandon, his fury apparent in every violent movement.

"Ha ha ha!" Jackson's laughter was deranged as he discovered a half-empty bottle of alcohol. He took a swig, the liquid spilling down his chin as he drank greedily.

"Drunkard…" Emma spat, her voice thick with disgust.

"What?!" Jackson whipped around, his eyes wild. "What did you call me?!" He grabbed Emma by the throat and hoisted her off the floor, his fingers like iron bands.

Emma's skin reddened, then darkened as the pressure cut off her blood flow. Her eyes bulged and filled with blood, and her struggles grew weaker. Jackson's grip only tightened, and finally, her movements ceased. With a final, contemptuous shove, he threw her lifeless body to the floor.

Jackson pulled out a chair and sat, straightening his disheveled hair. He fished a cigarette from his pocket, lighting it with deliberate, slow movements. The cigarette's ember glowed as he inhaled deeply, savoring the release.

A small, blue-eyed boy peeked around the corner, his face etched with terror. "Mom? Is everything okay?" he asked, his voice barely more than a whisper.

"Andrew! Get over here!" Jackson barked, pointing at the floor in front of him with a menacing gesture.

Andrew, paralyzed by fear, stood motionless. At just five years old, he was already familiar with the acrid stench of alcohol and cigarettes, and he instinctively shrank away from the sight of his father's rage.

"Is Mom okay?" Andrew's voice trembled, his gaze fixed on the lifeless body.

"She upset me," Jackson said, his tone cold and detached as he gestured with his cigarette. "You don't want to upset me too, do you?"

"No…" Andrew whimpered, shaking his head frantically.

Jackson grabbed Andrew's tiny hand, pressing the burning cigarette against his delicate skin.

"AAH!!! Daddy, it hurts! Stop it!" Andrew screamed, tears streaming down his face as he tried to pull away.

Jackson's face contorted into a nightmarish mask of rage. His eyes were dark voids, and his smile was a grotesque, predatory grin. His tongue flicked out between bared teeth as he pressed the cigarette deeper, the smoldering ember searing Andrew's flesh.

"ANDREW!!!" Jackson bellowed, an unnatural, almost inhuman voice echoing with twisted satisfaction as the cigarette burned into his son's skin.

Abruptly opening his eyes, Andrew looked around in fright. His pulse pounded in his ears, and his breathing was labored. The wet sheet and the porthole of the cabin reminded him of the torment of withdrawal.

"Hello, Mr. Brown…" the Devil greeted.

Andrew's body shuddered, a chill so intense that steam escaped from his mouth.

"Hello..." Andrew replied, pulling the blanket tighter around him.

"Abstinence... commendable, but I have very little faith in you," the Devil said, his tone dripping with insincerity.

Chattering from the cold, Andrew interrupted, "I didn't ask for two months of touring. I wanted phenomenal success."

"Isn't it phenomenal? Keep this up, and in two years, with smart investments, you'll afford three of these liners," the Devil replied, gesturing around the room.

"That's not what I asked for!" Andrew snapped, his voice tinged with desperation.

"You could have refused anytime and gone home. You signed contract after contract, received pay after pay, smiled for all of Europe with obsessive passion," the Devil grinned, eyes gleaming with malice.

Andrew closed his eyes, trying to calm the storm within. "I had a nightmare about my father. You said I wouldn't see them anymore..."

"You didn't see him. Andrew, you've lost yourself. Your body, thoughts, and actions don't belong to you anymore. Even your family—you don't want to spend time with them, right? I'm with them instead of you," the Devil taunted, his words slicing through Andrew's fragile resolve.

"I want to spend time with them! Doesn't this cruise prove anything?" Andrew's voice was shaky, on the brink of breaking.

"The cruise shows you travel by sea, but you don't spend time with them," the Devil replied smoothly. "Tomorrow is your last chance to use the envelope I gave you on the plane. Goodbye..." the Devil warned, his figure dissolving into the shadows.

"Hi," Sarah entered the room. "How are you?" she asked, looking at her husband wrapped in a blanket.

"Better, I think... What are your plans today?" Andrew asked, trying to shake off the lingering dread.

"We're thinking of going for a walk. The kids will be glad to see you," Sarah said quietly, her eyes searching his for a sign of the man she married.

Wiping his wet face and tidying himself up, Andrew replied, "I'll go with you today..."

—m—

After a long day spent with his family, Andrew felt the exhaustion weighing him down. But the sight of their smiles made every step worthwhile. With Sarah on his arm and Rene's hand in his, they walked along the sun-dappled beach in Greece. Little Noah wandered ahead, lost in his thoughts.

"Dad, will you be at my birthday party?" Noah asked hopefully, looking up at his father.

Andrew and Sarah exchanged a quick glance before he smiled and replied, "Of course! I wouldn't miss it for the world."

Rene hugged her father's leg, her smile as warm as the evening sun. Nearby, the strumming of an electric guitar drew cheers from a gathering crowd.

"Do you want to watch the concert?" Andrew asked the children.

"Yes, let's go!" they shouted in unison, their excitement infectious.

Sarah gave Andrew a cautious look, but he reassured her with a nod and led the family towards the music.

"Thank you very much!" the artist on stage called out to the crowd, his voice echoing over the waves.

As the speaker continued, Andrew turned to Sarah. "Do you remember when we struggled with our debts?"

"Yes," Sarah nodded, her expression thoughtful.

"Do you remember how I managed to pay them off? I made the right decision working with a producer, didn't I?" Andrew asked, his tone almost pleading.

Sarah frowned slightly, puzzled by his sudden introspection. "Wasn't Matthew the one who suggested it in the first place?"

"What does Matthew have to do with this?" Andrew snapped, his frustration evident.

"Matthew introduced you to Bradley," Sarah replied calmly.

Andrew looked away, his gaze fixed on the performer, his thoughts churning. "Who has done more for our family, me or Matthew?" he asked, his voice tight with emotion.

Sarah hesitated, sensing the tension. "Of course, you. Matthew helped us, yes, and I'm grateful to him for that," she said sincerely.

"Grateful to him, are you?" Andrew muttered, more to himself than to her. "Fine then..." He walked into the crowd, making his way to the stage.

The speaker interrupted his speech with an excited announcement: "Ladies and gentlemen, Andrew Brown is among us!"

The crowd quickly spotted Andrew and lifted him onto the stage. The speaker extended a hand, and Andrew pulled himself up, greeting the audience with a broad smile.

"Hello, Greece!" Andrew shouted. "Not long ago, I performed here. Do you want another performance?"

"Yes!" the crowd roared back, their energy palpable.

Andrew turned to the band and gave instructions. Moments later, the drummer set the rhythm, and the band, with Andrew as the vocalist, launched into a high-energy performance.

To a standing ovation, Andrew finished his set. "Thank you!" he called out, his heart racing with the thrill of the moment.

Noah and Rene clapped with delight, their faces glowing with pride. Sarah smiled, understanding the need he had to reconnect with his audience.

"Will you join us backstage?" the band invited Andrew.

"Sure," he agreed, signaling for his family to follow.

Backstage, amidst the camaraderie and laughter, the artists began to drink. "Mr. Brown?" one of the performers offered Andrew a glass of alcohol.

"No, thanks. I'm with my family," he declined, though the temptation was clear in his eyes.

The artist pulled out a small plastic bag of pills. "And for later?" he asked with a sly grin.

Andrew's gaze lingered on the bag, a battle waging within him.

"Hello everyone," Sarah greeted the artists, the children beside her.

Andrew quickly snatched the bag and pocketed it, forcing a smile. "Hi, dear," he said. "We should go. Have a great performance," he told the band.

As they walked along the beach at sunset, Andrew's thoughts kept drifting back to the pills in his pocket. But thinking about Sarah and her conditions, he reminded himself of his promise.

"Listen, can we stay here to rest?" Andrew suggested.

"Why?" Sarah asked, curiosity in her eyes.

"The cruise reminds me of... how ill I was," he softened his words, not wanting to worry the children.

"Daddy, were you very ill?" Rene asked, her small voice filled with concern.

"Yes, because I ate too much ice cream," Andrew said with a playful smile, glancing at Rene's half-eaten cone.

She grinned, her worries melting away like the ice cream in her hand.

"Okay, let's stay. For how long?" Sarah agreed, her eyes searching his for sincerity.

"As long as we want," Andrew replied, his smile genuine as he looked at his family, feeling a rare moment of peace.

—⁂—

In the evening, after renting a luxurious villa at an elegant Greek hotel, Sarah and Andrew, for the first time in ages, put the children to bed together. The room was softly lit, casting a warm glow on the children's faces.

"Dad, promise you'll never be ill again," Noah pleaded, his eyes wide with worry.

"I promise," Andrew replied, kissing his son on the forehead.

After wishing the children good night, the parents quietly closed the door and headed to their bedroom. As they walked, the comfortable silence between them felt heavy, filled with unspoken thoughts and lingering doubts. Andrew's phone vibrated in his pocket, making him flinch from the painful reaction of withdrawal.

"Hello?" he answered, his voice tinged with fatigue.

"Bradley?" Sarah whispered, her brow furrowing in concern.

Andrew nodded and gestured that he would join her soon. Sarah, expecting another disruption of their plans, locked herself in the bedroom, her heart sinking with resignation.

"Today's performance has gained a record number of views," Bradley announced, his voice exuding confidence. "Matthew will fly out to join you tomorrow. You'll perform every week and have more time with your family."

"Matthew? I scored those views myself," Andrew argued, his frustration growing.

"Nothing personal, but you'll get more views with both of you," Bradley interrupted.

Andrew clenched his jaw, pressing his temples with his hand. "Bradley, I'm not performing with Matthew. He kicked me off the stage!" he protested.

"It's either you perform with him, or you don't perform at all," Bradley retorted before hanging up.

In a fit of rage, Andrew kicked the nearest object, which happened to be Rene's beloved plush doll. The toy flew into a vase filled with roses, shattering it. The sound of breaking glass echoed through the house, a stark reminder of their fragile peace.

"Damn," he muttered, hurrying to clean up the mess. As he picked up the pieces, his hand slipped, and he fell onto a sharp shard of glass. The pain was immediate and intense, snapping him out of his anger.

"ANDREW!!!" an old, hoarse voice screamed in his mind.

His eyes snapped open, and he yanked his hand away from the shard, blood pouring from a deep cut between his thumb and wrist. Writhing in pain, he tried to stem the bleeding, but the dark, thick blood kept flowing.

Meanwhile, Sarah sat in an armchair by the bed, her mind racing with thoughts of what Andrew would say. She dialed a number on her phone, her hands trembling slightly.

"Hello, is this Shyla? I need your services. I'll pay you well..."

"I'm sorry, Shyla tragically passed away a few days ago," a voice responded, bringing a new wave of unease.

"What? What happened?" Sarah asked, her heart sinking.

The line went dead. Just then, Andrew entered the bedroom, noticing Sarah's anxious expression.

"Hey," he greeted her, trying to sound cheerful despite the tension in the air.

"Hi," Sarah replied, setting her phone aside, her eyes searching his face for answers.

Andrew sat down beside her and explained, "Matthew is coming tomorrow. We'll perform together every week, and I'll be with you the rest of the time."

Sarah remained silent, unsure how to feel, the weight of their strained relationship pressing down on her.

"Who were you talking to?" Andrew asked, curious but wary.

"Do you remember when I went to the fortune teller?" she reminded him, her voice soft.

"Yes..." he replied, sensing the shift in her mood.

"She died recently," Sarah said, still in shock.

Andrew took her hands and looked into her eyes. "What happened?"

"I don't know. They just said she died..." she trailed off, her thoughts elsewhere.

Andrew exhaled, looking down. "Sarah, I know you think I'll be away all the time. But this time, it's different. I'll perform once a week and spend the rest of the time with you. We'll put the kids to bed, go for walks, swim, and have fun together."

"Okay..." Sarah said, hoping for the best but bracing for disappointment, the spark in her eyes dimmed by doubt.

Andrew hugged her, stroking her back. "We're going to spend the best time together. Do you believe me?"

"Yes," Sarah smiled and kissed him, though the gesture felt more like a habit than a promise.

Despite the lingering tension, they quietly went to bed, both trying to hold onto a semblance of hope, their hearts heavy with the unspoken distance between them.

—⁂—

In a bar not far from his old apartment, Andrew drank furiously, hoping to obliterate the pain gnawing at his insides. He lost himself in hollow laughter, aimless chatter, and frequent trips to the restroom for more cocaine, his pockets growing lighter with each passing moment.

"Come on, go home, Andrew. Good night," the bartender said, his voice a mix of sympathy and exasperation.

"Okay…" Andrew mumbled, struggling to rise from his seat and stumbling out into the chill of the night.

The crisp air did little to clear his foggy mind as he patted his pockets, finding only emptiness. "Damn," he muttered with frustration and began the wobbly journey back to his old apartment.

His ascent up the stairs was almost mechanical. Fumbling at the door, his trembling fingers eventually managed to fit the key into the lock. As the door creaked open, a voice sliced through the darkness.

"I'm not surprised anymore!" Emma's voice cut through the air, sharp and accusing.

"Mom?!" Andrew's heart leaped, instantly clearing the fog of his intoxication. He yearned to collapse into her embrace, to share his life's tales and triumphs, to introduce her to his family. To him, she wasn't merely a mother but a beacon of lost warmth and solace. He felt a warmth spread through his chest, but it was quickly overshadowed by a dizzying darkness. His legs turned to jelly, and he crumpled to the floor, staring up at her.

"You missed your son's birthday," Emma's voice was laden with sorrow and reproach.

"I know… I was performing at a concert. I got him the best toy, and we went on a vacation…"

"Tuesday, Jackson… it's already Tuesday…" Emma's voice trembled with a mix of pain and weariness. "Why did you come?"

"What? I'm Andrew! Your son, do you remember me?" he pleaded, tears welling in his eyes.

"There is no money... I've paid my debts..." Emma's voice was firm but strained.

Confusion washed over Andrew as he lay on the floor. "Let me give you some money. How much do you need? I'll buy you a new house and cover all your debts. Mom, don't worry! Everything will be fine!" he assured, his voice cracking with desperation.

Without warning, a dark, writhing shadow emerged from a corner, moving with malevolent intent towards Emma. In a blur of motion, it hurled Andrew against the door, the impact jarring his head. He watched in frozen horror as the shadow loomed over his mother. Goosebumps crawled over his skin, and icy sweat broke out on his forehead. Emma remained blissfully unaware of the encroaching terror.

"Mom!" Andrew's voice was a desperate, strangled cry.

The shadow's face was a ghastly void, a swirling darkness where its eyes should be, a grotesque grin stretched wide. Its tongue flickered out from between bared, razor-sharp teeth. It reached Emma and struck her with brutal force, sending her crashing to the ground.

"Did you spend my money?!" the shadow roared, its voice a guttural snarl.

"I paid the debt!" Emma shouted, clutching her jaw, her voice breaking with pain.

Andrew, dazed and disoriented on the floor, struggled to process the scene. The blow to his head left his vision swimming, and his limbs felt heavy and unresponsive.

Growling with fury, the shadow seized Emma by her hair, dragging her violently toward the kitchen.

"No!!! Mom!!!" Andrew screamed, his voice raw with anguish as he dragged himself towards her.

"I know you're hiding it somewhere here…" the shadow rasped, its voice dripping with menace as it began to tear through the kitchen, ripping open shelves and throwing their contents aside in a frenzied search for money.

Emma, writhing in agony, watched helplessly as the shadow ransacked the kitchen. It found a half-full bottle of alcohol and drank greedily, savoring it like a fiendish nectar.

Andrew crawled toward his mother, his heart breaking with every painful step.

"Drunkard…" Emma spat at the shadow, her eyes blazing with hatred.

The shadow, its grin widening grotesquely, grabbed Andrew by the back and lifted him effortlessly. As Andrew's eyes met the shadow's, the entity seemed to merge with him. The shadow's dark, empty sockets and Andrew's own blue eyes fused into a terrifying amalgamation—two sets of eyes glaring out from the same face, one hollow and void, the other filled with a piercing, anguished blue. The effect was horrifying, a blend of darkness and agony that seemed to pierce the soul.

The shadow's presence seeped into Andrew's leg with a chilling cold that penetrated deep into the bone. The sensation was agonizing, a searing heat on the surface contrasted by a frigid numbness inside. It felt as if the shadow was not just touching but inhabiting Andrew's very being. The shadow seemed to flow into him like a dark mist, its essence intertwining with Andrew's, taking control with a cruel and suffocating grip.

"What?!" the shadow's voice thundered, echoing with a deep, menacing growl. It commanded Andrew's body, now a puppet to its will, directing him toward Emma. "What did you call me?!" it snarled, its hand tightening around Emma's throat, lifting her off the ground.

"What's happening?! Mom, I'm not doing this!!!" Andrew's voice cracked with panic as he felt the shadow's control tightening his hands around his mother's throat.

Andrew's mind screamed for control, but his body was a puppet to the shadow's will. He watched in torment as his hands squeezed, Emma's skin turning a fiery red, then deepening to a sickening blue. Her struggles grew weaker, her breathing shallow. Her life slipped away, and Andrew wept, his tears mingling with his mother's final breaths. Her body went limp, and he fell, broken, beside her.

"No!" Andrew sobbed, his face twisted in horror. The shock and despair were overwhelming. His body had betrayed him, killing his mother, the one person he had longed to reconnect with.

"Mom…" he choked out, his voice wracked with grief.

The shadow forced him to sit in a chair, pulling it out from the table. Andrew, his mind numb, straightened his disheveled hair, placing the bottle on the table by the shadow's command. He reached into his pocket, his hands trembling as he pulled out a pack of cigarettes and a lighter.

"No! I don't want to smoke… I don't want to smoke!!!" Andrew screamed, his voice a desperate plea as he fought against the cigarette in his hand.

From the corner, a small, blue-eyed boy peered out, his voice trembling. "Mom? Is everything okay?"

Andrew's heart shattered. "Noah, stay away! Please!!!"

The shadow, sitting with a cruel grin, pointed a long, bony finger at Noah, forcing him to comply. "Andrew! Come here!" it demanded, its voice a harsh rasp.

"I'm Andrew!" he shouted. "Noah, don't come near, no!!! Please!!!" Andrew screamed, his voice breaking with terror and despair.

Noah, despite his fear, edged closer to the shadow in Andrew's body. "What the fuck is happening?! Noah, stay away!!! Please forgive me!!!" Andrew's cries grew frantic, his heart aching with helplessness.

The shadow forced Andrew's hand to press the burning cigarette against Noah's small hand. "AAH!!! Ahh!!! Daddy! It hurts! Stop it!" Noah screamed, his voice cracking with pain and pleading.

Andrew's heart was shattered. He could only watch in torment as he was compelled to hurt his own child. The feeling of powerlessness and horror consumed him. He had just killed his mother and was now burning his son.

In Noah's tear-filled eyes, Andrew saw the reflection of his own face—hollow, with empty eye sockets, a grotesque grin, and a flickering tongue.

"ANDREW!!!" the shadow's voice boomed, driving Andrew to continue the torment.

"Aah!!!" Andrew's scream shattered the silence, his body jerking awake in a cold sweat. He lay on a tattered couch in an unfamiliar, dimly lit room. The walls were bare, save for a cracked mirror and a flickering fluorescent light that cast erratic shadows. The stark, sterile environment only deepened his disorientation.

"Where am I?! What is this place?! Sarah?! Noah?! Rene?!" Panic gripped him as he struggled to comprehend his surroundings. Each name a desperate cry for reassurance. The room's oppressive emptiness seemed to close in on him, heightening his fear.

"Hello, Andrew," came a calm, chilling voice from the shadows. The Devil lounged in the corner, his presence ominous and commanding.

"What the hell happened?! What the fuck?! How did I get here?!" Andrew's voice cracked, his breaths coming in frantic, uneven gasps. The Devil's presence was suffocating, an embodiment of the dread that had plagued Andrew's nightmare.

"Calm down..." The Devil's tone was smooth but cold. With a mere flick of his fingers, Andrew's jaw snapped shut with an audible click, silencing his cries.

"Speak calmly..." The Devil's gaze was unrelenting, his eyes reflecting a predatory gleam. The room seemed to pulse with his authority, every corner imbued with a menacing energy.

"I stopped smoking, drinking, and the drugs..." Andrew's voice broke, tears streaming down his face as he clutched his head. "Why couldn't I control myself? Where am I? What's wrong with my family?" His panic was palpable, his body trembling uncontrollably.

"You're in the dressing room. You have a concert with Matthew in twenty minutes. Your family is alive and well..." The Devil's voice was unnervingly calm, as if he were discussing the weather.

Andrew's face, though relieved momentarily, still bore the marks of his inner turmoil. His rapid breathing and twitching hands betrayed his struggle to regain composure. The room's sterile, cold atmosphere only intensified his sense of isolation.

"You think you've lost yourself to drugs, but that's not the whole truth. You loathe yourself, and that's your true burden..." The Devil's voice was a serpentine whisper, each word dripping with malevolent intent. His presence seemed to warp the air, filling it with a chilling dread.

"I love myself the most! I love singing, I love my hands, the air I breathe..." Andrew's voice wavered between desperation and denial, his eyes pleading for validation.

"I'll remind you to stay calm..." The Devil's tone grew sharper. "Is that what you truly are? Your name? Your hands? Your singing? Or is there something more?" The Devil's gaze was piercing, unsettling. "How blind you are! You are blind to your self-hatred!" Rising slowly, the Devil's movements were deliberate and terrifying, his figure a dark silhouette against the dim room.

Andrew's breaths were shallow, his body wracked with tremors. The Devil's words and presence seemed to warp reality itself, leaving Andrew in a state of disorienting fear. The oppressive cold of the room seeped into his bones, intensifying his dread.

"You don't need to try harder. You don't need that envelope anymore. The pills are in your back pocket. See you in hell..." The Devil's final words were a chilling promise, each syllable dripping with malicious intent. As he vanished, his ominous farewell lingered in the room like a dark cloud, amplifying Andrew's terror.

The emptiness that followed was suffocating. The cold, the fear, and the haunting words of the Devil left Andrew in a state of utter despair. Frantically, he pulled the pills from his back pocket, his hands shaking violently as he smashed them onto the coffee table. The sound of the pills breaking apart echoed through the room, amplifying his sense of panic.

He searched frenetically through a nearby locker, finding a dusty bottle of alcohol and a glass. His movements were desperate as he poured the alcohol, his hands trembling uncontrollably. Using the glass to crush the remaining pills, he filled it with the bitter liquid and collapsed face-first into the powdery residue. The burning sensation in his nostrils was sharp, and he coughed violently, his body writhing in agony.

As the drugs took effect, the crushing fear and cold began to dissipate, replaced by a numbing, hazy calm. Andrew sniffed more of the powder and drank the remaining liquid in a frantic bid for relief. His eyes became vacant, his mouth slightly open, and his vision blurred as he fell off the sofa, hitting his head on the table with a dull, resounding thud.

"What the hell, Andrew?! Damn it!" Matthew's voice was filled with alarm as he rushed to Andrew's side. He shook Andrew roughly, his concern evident in every line of his face.

Andrew mumbled incoherently, his speech slurred and his motor functions impaired. He reached out weakly, his attempts to communicate feeble and ineffective.

"What the fuck?! Are you high?! We have to perform in twelve minutes!!!" Matthew's frustration was palpable, his voice a mix of urgency and anger.

Noah and Rene burst into the room, their faces alight with joy as they presented bright red roses to their father. The joy quickly turned to horror as they saw Andrew lying on the floor, his face smeared with white powder, his mouth drooling uncontrollably.

"Children, go to your mother. We'll handle this..." Matthew's voice was a mixture of sorrow and authority. Rene's joyful cries turned to loud, frightened sobs as she dropped the roses and stared in terror at her father's state.

Sarah entered the room, her eyes widening in shock at the scene before her. The sight of her husband in disarray, Matthew's frantic efforts, and her children's distress struck her like a physical blow.

"Ah..." Andrew's eyes, glazed with drug-induced stupor, met Sarah's. Recognition flickered briefly before he was consumed by his own turmoil.

With a guttural scream of frustration and panic, Andrew shoved Matthew aside and leaned heavily against the table, struggling to stand on shaky legs. His face was contorted with a mix of fear and desperation.

"Children, we're leaving..." Sarah's voice was cold, her disappointment final.

Andrew reached out weakly toward Rene, but his balance failed him. He collapsed to the floor, his body crumpling as he watched his family walk away. The weight of his failures, the emptiness of his existence, and the echo of the Devil's words crushed him, leaving him utterly broken.

—⚹—

A girl with a bouquet of flowers stood among the frenetic crowd, eagerly awaiting the legendary duo. The pristine roses she clutched, the finest she could afford, were destined for her idol, Andrew. Dressed in her best white dress, she waited with bated breath, dreaming of this moment.

"Stay here..." Matthew instructed, pointing toward his drugged colleague backstage.

Andrew stood like a statue, his eyes half-closed and glazed. Cold sweat streamed down his face, his head spun uncontrollably, and his skin felt searingly hot on the outside while remaining unnervingly cold within. His black, buttoned-up shirt and trousers made him appear ominous and dismal.

"We perform for 20 minutes. When the next round of applause starts, we run out and sing the first song..." Matthew explained, frustration etched in his voice. He placed Andrew's guitar beside him. "Here's your guitar. Don't forget it. I'll be coming out from the other side of the stage, remember?" He bore into Andrew's vacant eyes.

"Yes..." Andrew managed to mumble, his tongue thick and slow.

Matthew hurried backstage, preparing for the performance.

The girl with the bouquet, brimming with anticipation, began clapping loudly, her excitement mirrored by the crowd.

Matthew ran out first to greet the audience. Realizing he was alone on stage, he cast a furious glare toward the side where Andrew was meant to appear.

Andrew, grinning vacantly, stumbled onto the stage, oblivious to his missing guitar. An assistant rushed forward with the instrument.

"Sir, your guitar," the assistant said, offering it to Andrew.

In his drugged stupor, Andrew barely acknowledged the assistant and continued to wave absentmindedly to the crowd.

"Sir…" The assistant stepped closer and handed the guitar to him again.

Andrew strapped on the guitar and staggered to the microphone stand, his movements sluggish and erratic. He adjusted the mic with labored effort. Finally, Matthew signaled for the performance to begin.

The crowd erupted, jumping, singing, and stomping in rhythm with the music. The girl with the bouquet was ecstatic, having waited months for this moment.

During Andrew's solo, he played fifteen notes wrong, yet the music was flawless. Realizing that Matthew had turned off his guitar and switched to a pre-recorded soundtrack, Andrew's face twisted into a mask of pure hatred as he glared at his colleague.

As the song ended, the crowd cheered, including the girl with the roses.

"Thank you!" Matthew shouted into the microphone. "The next song means a lot…"

The performance was abruptly interrupted by a deafening crash as Andrew smashed his guitar against the stage. He struck it again and again with frenzied force until it shattered into splinters. Matthew stared in exasperated disbelief. The crowd fell silent, their initial excitement replaced by stunned silence.

The girl in the white dress, initially cheering, began to clap hesitantly. The crowd slowly picked up the ovation, albeit uncertainly.

Andrew, still in a drug-induced haze, grabbed the microphone from the stand and stumbled toward Matthew.

"I was deceived... It was all a soundtrack..." Andrew slurred into the microphone, yet no sound came from the stage.

Unbeknownst to him, both the microphone and guitar were off. Andrew had been miming the performance while Matthew sang. Laughing maniacally, Andrew threw the microphone aside and seized Matthew's mic.

"My microphone was off..." Andrew mumbled incoherently, still laughing.

Matthew began to resist, pushing Andrew away gently. But Andrew, with unrestrained strength, yanked the microphone and lost his balance. He collapsed onto the stage, falling before the bewildered audience.

"Wow" echoed hollowly through the stunned crowd.

"I'm fine!" Andrew declared awkwardly, raising his hands in a misguided show of triumph.

"Boo!" Matthew and the audience yelled in unison, their voices laced with anger and disappointment.

Andrew, his high consuming him, moved with jerky, unsteady motions. Each step was a battle against his wavering balance. His eyes, bloodshot and vacant, revealed the depth of his detachment from reality. His body, trembling with exertion, seemed to be on autopilot as he approached Matthew with cold, unfeeling hatred.

Swinging the microphone with all his might, Andrew struck Matthew violently on the head. The sound of the impact reverberated through the venue, blood splattering across the audience and staining Andrew's face. Matthew crumpled onto the stage, a growing pool of blood forming around his head, the pink and red droplets vividly staining the microphone.

The stage fell into a deathly silence, punctuated only by the sharp, piercing beep of the fallen microphone. Andrew stood motionless, his eyes half-closed, a vacant expression frozen on his face. Cold sweat drenched him, and his mind spun in confusion and horror.

The girl in the front row dropped her bouquet, her expression frozen in fear. She glanced between Andrew, lost in his drug-induced stupor, and Matthew, lying in a pool of blood. Her once-immaculate dress was now stained with the blood of her second favorite artist, and she stood paralyzed by the horrific spectacle

—m—

On a poorly lit street, a man staggered as far as possible from the performance venue. Rapid breathing, dizziness, and body pain from his frantic escape only exacerbated Andrew's torment. Each step felt like an agonizing reminder of the wreckage he had left behind—his career, his friendship, his reputation.

"ANDREW!!!" A hoarse scream cut through the darkness.

The sound jolted him, and he tumbled to the side of the road. His pulse thundered as he scrambled to his feet, heart racing. He checked his pockets in a daze. In his back left pocket, he found an envelope given to him by the Devil on the plane. With trembling hands, he opened it and saw the address.

"It's just a few blocks from here..." he muttered, clinging to the hope of finding some solace.

As Andrew approached the address, the surroundings shifted to quaint, dimly lit houses. He teetered to a stop in front of one particular house, his heart hammering in his chest. Through a window, he saw a familiar face—Grace. Her brown hair and gentle features were a stark contrast to the chaos he had just escaped. His heart ached with a mix of longing and regret.

Andrew started to walk towards the house but froze when he glanced at his bloodstained right hand. The red streaks on his skin were a grim reminder of the violence he had unleashed on Matthew. The sight was almost surreal, a brutal juxtaposition to the tranquil image of Grace.

"And what should I tell her?" he wondered, feeling a swell of despair. "What's happening? I don't even know if Matthew is alive. And Sarah? What's wrong with her? Grace?!"

As he watched Grace, a torrent of memories and emotions surged through him. He remembered their school days, the innocence of their first kiss, and the dreams they once shared. He envisioned a life where they went to the same university, married, and built a family together. The thought of Grace waiting at home, their children laughing and playing, filled him with a deep, aching sorrow. It was a future that had slipped through his fingers, replaced by a reality he no longer recognized or wanted.

Andrew's heart clenched with regret and yearning. He realized he no longer desired a life with Sarah. He had never shared his deepest fears and nightmares with Sarah—not because she couldn't understand, but because he didn't want to burden her with his darkness. He knew, deep down, he would have opened his soul to Grace. He would have shared everything—the Devil's deal, the drug addiction, the suffocating weight of his despair. He imagined doing everything in his power to make her happy, to find redemption and peace.

"Sarah... I love her too... our children..." flashed painfully through his mind.

Grace, lost in her task of cutting flowers from the balcony, appeared serene and content. Andrew felt a profound sense of harmony watching her, a stark contrast to the turmoil he was living. When Grace noticed the man in the black shirt standing on the side of the road, her confusion was evident. She seemed to recognize him but continued with her task. Andrew froze, terrified she might recognize him. Grace's abrupt realization made her accidentally cut the stem of a flower, which fell to the ground. She looked down at the fallen flower, then back at where Andrew stood—but he had already fled.

Unable to bear the weight of his own despair, Andrew bolted away, running three blocks before he finally stopped. Overwhelmed, he reached into his right back pocket, pulling out a bag of pills. With desperation clawing at him, he swallowed several pills dry, the gritty texture and harsh taste making his throat burn. He forced himself to swallow, wincing as the fragments scraped painfully against his throat. His body shivered uncontrollably, but a twisted smile spread across his face as the drug's effects began to numb his senses. With pupils constricting to mere pinpricks, he staggered towards home, the last remnants of his sanity slipping away with each step.

—⟊—

Sure, I'll intensify the emotions and deepen the descriptions even further.

After stumbling on the asphalt a couple of times, smoking a few cigarettes, and perhaps drinking something else, Andrew miraculously reached the villa. Each step was a battle, his body swaying and uncooperative. His mind was a chaotic whirlwind, filled with fragmented memories and a single haunting phrase: "See you in hell..."

"Can the Devil deceive? Well, of course he can, he's a tempter! He lied to Adam! Or Eve? He lied to someone... Right? Was it said that he lied? Is it tempting to cheat?" Andrew muttered, his voice trembling as he tried to rationalize his fears.

His thoughts were as erratic as his legs. He kept glancing over his shoulder, expecting the shadow from his nightmare to leap out at him from the darkness. Every flicker of a shadow, every rustle of leaves, made his heart pound with terror. Finally, when he reached the door of the villa, Andrew took out his keys and tried with incredible diligence to put them into the lock. His hands trembled violently, making it a challenge. Opening the door, he was met by his wife. Her husband's tired eyes, puffy face, heavy breathing, and small specks of sweat on his forehead... The symptoms were obvious.

"I'm not surprised anymore!" Sarah began angrily.

Andrew's eyes widened. Fear enveloped him like a cold blanket. A repeating scene from his nightmare surfaced in front of him, only now his wife was standing just like his mother, saying the same thing. He kept glancing sharply to the side, trying to predict where the shadow from his dream would come from.

"Look at me!" Sarah shouted at him.

"Wait!" Andrew shouted, pouncing on his wife as if protecting her. "Look over there!" he pointed at one of the many walls of the villa. "Something is coming out now..." Andrew whispered in horror, his voice trembling.

Sarah looked warily at the point her husband was pointing at, waiting for something to appear. Andrew's heart pounded in his chest, and his breath quickened. Every flicker of a shadow made him jump, convinced it was the harbinger of his doom.

Sarah broke away from his embrace. "Are you crazy?! Are you hallucinating or something?!" she shouted.

"No! Look! Look!" Andrew pointed at the wall in fear, his eyes wide and wild.

"Stop it! Nothing's there!" Sarah came close to him.

Andrew, remembering that he was high, began to recall what happened. His mind raced with disjointed images and sounds, the concert, the guitar smashing, Matthew's bloodied face.

"The concert. Guitar. A broken guitar... Matthew. Microphone... Blood... Is Matthew dead?! Is he alive at all?!" thoughts flooded his mind.

"Sarah! Please forgive me..." Andrew fell into his wife's lap, hugging her waist. "I lost my temper... I really didn't mean to... I..." Tears streamed down his face, and he glanced around the room, still half-expecting the shadow to emerge from a corner.

Sarah tried to push him away at first, but when she saw the tears, she couldn't help but provide support.

"What happened?" Sarah asked in a neutral tone.

"I can explain... honestly..." Andrew defended himself, looking into his wife's eyes, but constantly darting his gaze around, terrified the shadow would appear any moment.

Dring, Dring. Sarah's phone rang. She took her phone out of her pocket and looked at who was calling. "Grace." Her face froze. After all these years... Grace was calling Sarah. Childhood friend... Sister... Memories of their friendship flashed through her mind. She showed her husband who was calling. Andrew seemed to freeze, not knowing whether to pounce on the phone or try to explain that he didn't know he was coming to her.

"Hello," Sarah answered the phone quite calmly.

"Sarah... hi," Grace's warm voice was heard.

Sarah shed tears at the sound of her friend's voice and moved away from her husband. Andrew looked at his wife, unsure of what to do. His mind was a storm of conflicting emotions, but underlying everything was the relentless fear of the shadow.

"No… What will she say? Will she scream? Will she even talk to me?"

"Grace... I... I'll call you back," Sarah said, going back to her husband.

After dropping the phone, Sarah tearfully approached Andrew, looked into his eyes, and asked, "You met Grace?" her voice trembling.

A lump rose in Andrew's throat. It was difficult to speak. What could he say?

"What do you mean I met her? I saw her, yes. But I didn't meet her. I saw her by chance..." Andrew said, still glancing nervously around the room.

"By chance?! In Greece?! And right in front of her house?! After that photo?!" Sarah desperately doubted her husband's words.

"Yes... by chance. I can explain everything… Listen, please..."

"Explain!" Sarah interrupted.

"You can ask her! I was as surprised as she was! I even ran away when she noticed me!" Andrew shouted, getting up from his knees, his voice rising with panic.

"What?! Have you been following her?!" Sarah asked in shock.

"No! I happened to see her earlier, passing by her house! Ask her!!! I was walking there after the concert!" Andrew defended himself, his voice trembling.

"Your concert..." Sarah said, her voice filled with anger. "What the fuck happened?! You sent Matthew to the ICU!!!" she screamed.

"Don't yell at me!!!" Andrew exploded, his fear morphing into anger as he approached his frightened wife.

Sarah stepped back, terrified of her husband's sudden outburst. Andrew was just as shocked by his own reaction. He had never screamed like that before. It was as if someone else had taken over his voice.

"Don't do that..." Sarah said seriously, her fear evident.

"Don't raise your voice at me..." Andrew pointed a threatening finger at his wife.

"Andrew... you lost it! We agreed... You've been in bed for 15 days, for what? For this?" Sarah's voice broke with pain.

Andrew frowned sadly, squatting down and clutching his temples.

"It wasn't me..." Andrew shook his head. "I can explain it too, it will sound silly, but it's true.... I want to tell you the truth about everything..." he said sadly.

"I'm listening..." Sarah said, crossing her arms.

After a moment of thought, Andrew decided to tell her everything. Looking into his wife's eyes, he began, "Do you believe in the Devil?" he asked quietly.

"What? The Devil?" Sarah asked, not understanding.

"Yes. The Devil..." Andrew replied seriously.

Sarah threw her arms up in exasperation. "What now? You sold your soul to the Devil and it's all because of that?" she asked mockingly.

"Don't laugh at it..." Andrew said seriously. "All of it..." he waved his hand around the villa. "All of this! Thanks to me!" he pointed at himself.

Sarah's phone rang, interrupting the argument.

"Yes?" she answered worriedly.

"What is it? Do you have to run again? Don't you want to talk to your husband?!" Andrew raised his voice, not controlling his thoughts and body.

Sarah's face darkened. "Thank you..." she said, hanging up. "Matthew died of a hematoma in his head..." she burst into tears.

Andrew grabbed his head in panic with both hands.

"You know, I don't care what you say, I don't care about your reasons... I can't do this anymore..." Sarah said sadly.

"Andrew, I'm filing for divorce..." she said, her voice breaking.

Andrew froze in shock, staring into Sarah's tear-filled eyes. The room seemed to spin around him, the walls closing in as her words sank in. The rage inside him simmered, threatening to boil over.

"What do you mean, a divorce? Why? How can you? After everything?" he stammered, his voice trembling.

"You're a murderer, a drug addict, and an alcoholic," Sarah said, her voice breaking. "The lawyer said you'd be very lucky if you ever saw my children..."

"Your children?! Your children?!" Andrew's voice rose to a scream, the demon inside him clawing its way to the surface. His eyes darted around, half-expecting the shadow to emerge from the darkness and envelop him.

Sarah turned away from him, her voice cold and resolute. "My children... You're either at work or lying in bed like a drug addict..."

Andrew's rage erupted. He lunged forward, grabbing her arm and spinning her around. Sarah slapped him hard across the cheek. The sting ignited a feral rage in Andrew, his face contorting into a hateful snarl. He grabbed her by the throat, his grip tightening as he screamed, "These are my children! Stupid parasite, what have you got? What did you do?! Get out of my house!!!" He shoved her back with such force that she crashed into the wall, leaving bruises on her neck.

Leaving the crying woman, Andrew stormed into the bedroom. Desperation clawed at him as he rummaged through his back pocket, finding his crumpled package. Frantically opening it, he found no pills. Enraged, he threw the bag aside, his eyes catching sight of his daughter's plush toy. Tearing it apart, a bag of white powder fell out. With trembling hands, he carefully poured the contents onto the table and began to inhale. His nose burned, and tears streamed down his face, but he continued, needing the escape.

"Look at you…" Sarah's voice came from the doorway, a mix of laughter and sobs. "You're sick, Andrew! I will never let the children near you!" She cried, her eyes filled with disgust and sorrow.

"You won't let me, huh?" Andrew turned to her, his voice a hoarse growl. "These are my children!!!" He pounded his chest with a powder-stained hand.

"No!" Sarah screamed, blocking his path as he tried to leave the bedroom.

Andrew laughed, a cold, bitter sound, and punched her hard in the stomach. Sarah collapsed, gasping for breath, unable to scream. She watched in horror as her husband headed for their children's room.

"Wake up, we're leaving…" Andrew said, his voice a harsh whisper as he entered Noah and Rene's room.

Noah, already awake and trembling, had heard the entire argument. "What's wrong with Uncle Matthew?" the boy asked, his voice small and scared.

Andrew lifted the sleeping Rene out of bed, glaring at his son. "He's not your uncle, I'm your father… Come on, we're leaving…"

"Where are we going? Is Mom okay?" Noah asked, his anxiety mounting.

Andrew ignored him, putting Rene on his right shoulder and pulling Noah out of bed with his other hand.

"Dad, what happened?" Noah struggled to keep up, his voice quivering.

Andrew didn't respond. Noah saw his mother on the floor, clutching her stomach and crying.

"Andrew, you're a monster…" Sarah's voice was weak but filled with pain.

"Dad, what's wrong with Mom?!" Noah began to cry, noticing the blood on his father's thumb. "You're bleeding…"

"Stupid thing… wanted a divorce…" Andrew muttered.

"Daddy, I don't want to go…" his son pleaded, looking at his struggling mother.

Rene, silent and terrified, watched the scene with shocked eyes.

Outside, he put his daughter in the front seat and dragged Noah into the back, strapping them in roughly. As he got behind the wheel, he saw Sarah running out of the house, trying to block the car. Laughing maniacally, Andrew floored the gas pedal, aiming to knock her down.

"Rene! Noah!" Sarah screamed, the headlights reflecting her terrified face.

At the last moment, Sarah managed to dive out of the way, hitting the ground hard. Gritting her teeth against the pain, she pulled out her phone and frantically called the police.

"Dad, I'm scared!" Rene's small voice trembled.

Andrew ignored the crying children, focusing on putting as much distance as possible between them and the villa. Seeing the flashing blue and red lights in his rearview mirror, he pressed harder on the gas, his heart pounding.

The car swerved dangerously around corners, the children's screams blending with the wail of sirens. Andrew's knuckles turned white on the steering wheel, his eyes wide and unblinking. In a desperate attempt to lose the police, he took a sharp turn at high speed. The car fishtailed, lost traction, and crashed into a lamppost. The impact triggered the airbags, slamming into Andrew's face and chest. Rene and Noah cried out, clutching their stomachs where the seat belts cut into them.

"Hurry up! Take the kids to the ambulance..." a policeman shouted to his partner as he opened Andrew's door.

"AAARGH!" Andrew roared, struggling against the police officer.

The officer pulled out a Taser and neutralized Andrew, his body convulsing before slumping. He watched helplessly as his terrified children were carried away by police cars.

Silence engulfed him, punctuated only by the sound of his ragged breathing. After being cuffed and placed in the back of a police car, Andrew's mind spiraled.

"Devil... please help me... I beg you... I beg you..." he muttered, his voice cracking.

Suddenly, the front tire of the car exploded, sending it careening out of control. The car flipped, the world spinning before Andrew's eyes. When it came to a stop, he found himself unharmed amidst the wreckage. The officer lay unconscious, bleeding. Andrew grabbed the keys, freed himself from the cuffs, and stumbled out, running towards the hospital, desperate to find his children.

—⚏—

His head buzzed with a cacophony of regrets and self-loathing. Andrew replayed everything that had happened, cursing himself under his breath.

"Divorce... I can't believe it... How could she? I killed Matthew... I don't even know what's wrong with the kids..."

Regret and hatred intertwined in his heart. As Andrew trudged down the street, the early morning light cast long shadows that seemed to mock him. Combing an open cut on his left thumb, he muttered curses, his voice hoarse and desperate.

"Shit!" Andrew let out a loud, hoarse scream, the sound echoing down the deserted street.

"Hey!" a man called out, his voice rough like sandpaper. "Come here!" the old man pointed with a trembling hand.

Andrew turned towards the voice and recognized his father, a figure from a past he had tried to forget.

"The hell are you doing here?!" Andrew raised his voice, anger flaring in his eyes.

"Where is your family? Why would you kill him? Are you high? You goddamn coward!!" the old man shouted, coming close to Andrew, his eyes wild with fury.

"Who are you to me?!" Andrew pushed the old man away, the smell of cigarettes and despair mingling in the air. "You can't quit on your own," he sneered, alluding to the stench of stale smoke.

"I haven't had a family for a long time! And I only smoke! And what about you?! Are you really that stupid?!" the old man croaked, hitting himself on the head with a clenched fist, his voice cracking with rage.

"You don't have a family because you ruined it…" Andrew snapped, his words cutting like a knife.

Rage consumed the old man. With a guttural roar, he lunged at Andrew and started beating him. His fists flew, each punch fueled by years of pent-up anger and bitterness. Andrew fell to the sidewalk, and the old man straddled him, continuing to pummel his chest. Blow after blow, the sound of fists meeting flesh echoed in the still morning air. Blood splattered, staining the concrete and the old man's knuckles, but he didn't stop. The old man lost track of time, his fury driving him to the brink of madness.

"You ruined my family…" the old man muttered, his breath ragged as he looked down at the bloody, motionless body beneath him.

He fumbled in his pocket with shaking hands, pulling out a pack of cigarettes. Extracting one with bloodied fingers, he placed it in his mouth. Reaching into his back pocket, he retrieved a lighter and flicked it on. The flame sputtered but didn't catch. He tried again, and again, growing more agitated with each failed attempt. The lighter refused to work, mirroring his own impotent rage.

Andrew, unable to say anything, could only watch. His body was numb after all the substances from the previous night, and he felt no pain. As he observed his father trying to light a cigarette, he remembered how the old man had left a burn on his arm, a cruel mark of their shared history.

Cursing under his breath, the old man tossed the lighter into the street and rifled through Andrew's pockets until he found another one. Finally, he lit the cigarette and took a deep drag, savoring the harsh smoke as it burned his lungs. He stepped over Andrew's bloodied body and walked down the street, the smoke curling behind him like a ghostly trail.

Andrew's gaze fixed on his father's left hand. He noticed a familiar scar on the old man's thumb, a scar that mirrored the fresh cut on his own hand. Confusion and a flicker of recognition crossed his face.

"What is it?" Andrew tried to focus on the old man's left hand.

As the old man walked away, Andrew's mind raced. He struggled to understand who the man standing over him was. The old man's scar was the same size, in exactly the same place as Andrew's.

"Who are you?" Andrew managed to croak out, his voice barely audible.

The old man did not hear him, continuing to walk on until he disappeared from sight, leaving Andrew lying on the sidewalk, drenched in blood and bewilderment.

———

20 years later…

"For all this time, I've been searching for someone to blame for everything that's happened," said a well-groomed elderly man, leaning against a wall in a narrow alley. His voice was heavy, each word laden with years of regret and unanswered questions.

"Why would you want to see the day of your death?" a middle-aged man beside him asked, his tone edged with curiosity and a hint of disbelief.

Andrew's gaze was fixed on a filthy, disheveled old man sprawled on a cardboard box. The stench of cheap alcohol clung to the air, mixing with the oppressive gloom of the alley.

Turning to the Devil, Andrew said, "I blamed you... myself... my father... the producer... Matthew... even Sarah." His voice wavered between anger and deep sorrow. "But over time, I realized that blaming others was futile. You have to accept things as they are and move on." He took a deep breath, his expression softening. "I've spent my life consumed by hatred… I don't hate myself anymore."

The Devil, watching the old man in the alley with extreme interest, chuckled darkly. "You humans are endlessly fascinating. You cling to meaningless concerns, obsess over trivialities, and yet you find some perverse form of harmony in it all," he said, his grin revealed in the dim light.

"Yes, harmony might seem meaningless, but it's something I need," Andrew replied, holding a blanket tightly as if it were a symbol of his last vestiges of hope.

The Devil extended a predatory hand towards the filthy old man, and Andrew stepped forward, leaving his teacher alone.

Gently covering the stinking old man with the blanket, Andrew whispered, "I accept you." His voice was steady, carrying a sense of resignation. He then turned away, leaving the Devil to carry out his dark work.

"Good afternoon, Mr. Brown," a middle-aged man greeted the old man with icy detachment.

The old man, confused and groggy, mumbled, "Huh?"

The Devil exhaled slowly and snapped his fingers. Instantly, the old man's drunken stupor lifted; his eyes fluttered open, and he shivered under the blanket, feeling the cold seeping into his bones.

"Hello," Andrew said, his voice barely audible as he watched in dread.

"It is time," the Devil said, his tone cold and final as he extended his hand to the old man, who stared at it in a mix of fear and resignation.

"Time for what?" Andrew asked, his voice a tremulous whisper.

The old man's mind scrambled to recall his last encounter with the Devil. Fragments of terror and dread pieced together, making his heart race.

"The last time I saw you, you told me 'see you in hell…'" Andrew said, his fear palpable as he looked at the Devil, realizing the full horror of his situation.

"Yes… the time has come," the Devil replied, his voice cold and devoid of empathy.

Andrew extended a trembling hand towards the middle-aged man, shaking it. In an instant, a blinding fire enveloped them, and Andrew recoiled in terror. They found themselves in a dimly lit hall, lined with an array of doors. From each door came sounds of anguish—crying, screaming, maniacal laughter—each noise more disturbing than the last.

"Where are we?" Andrew asked, his voice choked with fear as he sank to the floor, overwhelmed by the nightmarish surroundings.

The Devil's gaze remained icy and unmoved. "Hell," he replied laconically, the word echoing through the desolate hall like a death knell.

The dimly lit hall echoed with the muffled sounds of footsteps, a chilling reminder of the souls that roamed its depths. A middle-aged man emerged from the shadows, moving with a smooth yet confident gait. His highly polished business shoes, gray sweater, and trousers gave him a classically simple appearance. But his proudly raised head, precise steps, and free movements exuded a sense of ownership over this infernal realm.

As he moved through the corridor, sounds seeping through the doors lining the hall interrupted the dead silence. At first glance, it seemed as though he was walking a straight path. However, the corridor flowed in serpentine curves, like the winding coils of a snake. The doors stood at different levels, each one exuding a different aura of torment. Bitter, guttural crying came from one, manic laughter from another, and quiet screams from a third. The further he walked, the more varied and intense the sounds became, yet he continued with unwavering confidence.

Finally, he stopped at a particular door and checked his watch. The time showed 5:59. Patiently waiting for the last minute, surrounded by muffled voices and the heavy, oppressive air, he watched as the clock moved forward. At precisely 6:00, he knocked on the door.

"Come in..." a hoarse, broken voice responded from the other side.

Entering the room, the man was met by an elderly, unkempt figure. It was difficult to determine his age; he could have been 60, 90, or thousands of years old. His clothes were torn and filthy, his hands wrapped in old, dirty bandages, and his feet covered by worn-out, leaky shoes. He reeked of alcohol and stale sweat, his skin pocked and yellowed from years of substance abuse. A scar on his left thumb and a cigarette burn on his hand. Andrew was sitting on an old wooden chair, looking at the Devil.

The man briefly assessed the room. Empty glass bottles and used syringes littered the floor, and the air was thick with the stench of decay. A dim lamp on the ceiling cast a sickly yellow light, attracting aimlessly-flying moths. A worktable stood to one side, covered in crumpled paper and a vase of wilted flowers. In the center of the room sat the old man, glued to a wooden chair, his eyes bloodshot and filled with a mix of hatred and despair.

"How are you?" the man asked coldly, his voice carrying an unsettling authority. The voice of a man who is absolutely confident in himself, who knows and understands everything and seems to have lived on Earth for thousands of years.

"Can't you see?" the old man responded blankly, his voice a gravelly rasp. "Miserable..."

Grinning with a hint of malice, the man turned his attention to the table. "Why don't you change the flowers?"

"What's the point of changing them? They'll wither in a day or two anyway," the old man snapped, his voice filled with bitterness. "Speaking of days, how long have I been here? I don't remember the first day in this damn room. I've lost track of time long ago..."

"What's the point of knowing? Knowing won't change anything anyway," the man repeated, his tone dripping with irony.

The old man looked down, his expression a mix of anger and resignation.

"Perhaps you would like to know... how to change your life?" the man suggested aloofly, his eyes glinting with a sinister promise as he circled the room.

The old man's once dull eyes filled with a flicker of hope and childish delight. "Yes! Please! Tell me how!" he pleaded in a hoarse voice, throwing himself at the feet of the newcomer, his desperation palpable.

"I doubt you will be able to do it. You'll probably give up not even on the tenth, but on the second attempt," the man explained coldly, his words cutting deep.

"I'll do anything! I swear!" the old man begged, his voice trembling with desperation.

The man looked disinterestedly towards the exit and walked to the door.

"I can do it! Give me a chance! I beg you!" the old man cried out, his voice cracking.

The man looked down at the old man and said, "Okay, listen carefully," his tone serious and commanding.

The old man nodded vigorously, staring at him expectantly on his knees, his eyes wide with hope.

"First, clean up the room and change the flowers in the vase," the man instructed, his voice echoing with a chilling finality.

Andrew rose from his knees, each movement slow and heavy as he approached the table. The vase, with its withered flowers, seemed to mock his hope. Imagining fresh roses, he watched as they materialized in his hands. Carefully, he removed the old, decayed flowers and replaced them with the vibrant new ones, his hands trembling as he tried to cling to the last vestige of hope.

"Sit down," the Devil commanded in a smooth, authoritative tone, gesturing to a chair with an almost languid grace.

Andrew sank into the chair, his posture a mix of defeat and readiness, awaiting whatever the Devil would say.

"You could always move upstairs," the Devil continued, pointing toward the ceiling. "But remember, the flowers will wither as soon as you leave hell. You'll have exactly fifty-seven minutes to reach the top. If the flowers are withered, you won't make it."

"How do I do this?" Andrew asked, desperation lacing his voice.

The Devil's smile widened, revealing a predatory edge. "It's simple. Just imagine the place and time you want to be."

"But I imagined it, and nothing happened..." Andrew said, frustration creeping in.

"Were the flowers withered or fresh?" The Devil's grin grew wider, clearly relishing Andrew's struggle.

Andrew's eyes widened with realization. "I could have left all this time... just by changing the flowers?"

"Yes," the Devil confirmed, his tone dripping with disdain. "Graves, birthday gifts, flowers—they carry vital energy. By placing them on graves, you channel that energy to temporarily escape this place."

A wild joy erupted on Andrew's face as he pictured himself alone on a sunlit beach. In an instant, the room erupted in searing, hellish flames. The fire was not merely bright; it roared and writhed with infernal fury, casting grotesque shadows that seemed to claw at the walls. Andrew was engulfed, his form twisting in the flames as they writhed like living serpents.

The Devil's free widened as he settled into a wooden chair, awaiting the soul of the sinner. As the flower's vibrancy faded Andrew reappeared, hovering in the air for a brief moment before crashing violently to the floor. The hellish fire had left the room dark and oppressive, with the smoke curling like the whispers of lost souls.

"What is this?! No!!!" Andrew screamed, his voice filled with terror and disbelief as he found himself back in hell.

"You can try again," the Devil taunted, his voice a cold, mocking echo in the gloom. "Change the flowers and attempt once more."

"It's pointless," Andrew cried, despair thick in his voice. "I'm never leaving here... How do I get to heaven?"

"Reaching heaven is far more arduous. You must purge yourself of your sins," the Devil explained, his tone devoid of sympathy. "You took the life of your best friend, wronged your wife, abused substances, and lived in self-loathing. Most tragically, you never allowed yourself to live in true harmony."

"How do I rid myself of sin?" Andrew's voice trembled with dread.

"Go back in time and convince your younger self to embrace harmony. When did your difficult period with Sarah start?"

Andrew stood and moved to change the flowers again, his face a mask of determination mixed with fear. "Why Sarah? I wanted to be with Grace."

"Responsibility, Andrew. You married Sarah before God," the Devil laughed, though his eyes remained cold.

"Ah, so that's how it works..." Andrew said, realization dawning. "The producer! The day Matthew took me to the producer!"

"Why did he take you there?" the Devil asked, his gaze piercing.

"To earn money..." Andrew admitted, guilt evident in his tone.

"Then go back to that day," the Devil said, pointing at his watch. "I'll be waiting."

The hellish flames roared to life once more, their intensity almost unbearable. Andrew was engulfed, the flames surging with a violent heat that seemed to claw at his very essence. As he vanished from the room, the flowers withered rapidly, their energy expended.

When the flames subsided, Andrew reappeared, coughing and disoriented. He looked around, his eyes wide with disbelief.

"He thought... the young me thought I was homeless!" Andrew said indignantly.

"Get yourself together and try again, and again, until you convince your younger self to live a life of pleasure and harmony," the Devil instructed, his tone laced with dark amusement.

"I'll have to give up all my bad habits..." Andrew said, his voice quivering.

"Do you truly want to remain here forever?" the Devil asked, his gaze cold and unforgiving.

"No!" Andrew exclaimed, desperation sharp in his voice.

The Devil's smile widened as he rose from his chair. "Good luck then. You have all the time you need, but remember one rule: no one must know you are Andrew."

"Understood," Andrew said, steeling himself as he changed the flowers once more.

"Excellent!" the Devil said, his voice with malicious glee. As Andrew disappeared into the infernal flames once again, the Devil's laughter echoed behind him, leaving the sinner to face his eternal torment.

EPILOGUE

"Goodbye, Grace," the Devil said, crossing her name out of his notebook with a final, chilling stroke.

"Goodbye," the girl replied dejectedly, her voice barely above a whisper.

Grace left the office feeling empty, her mind a swirling vortex of despair and confusion.

"It's Grace, right?" the assistant girl smiled, her smile not quite reaching her eyes.

Grace looked at the girl sitting at the table. The name on the tag read: "Lilith."

Grace forced a smile, her heart heavy with sorrow.

"How are you? Did it get easier?" Lilith asked sympathetically, though her tone was void of genuine concern.

"I don't know..." Grace replied, looking down, her voice tinged with hopelessness.

Lilith smiled and said, "Don't worry, dear, everything will be fine... When would you like to schedule your next session?"

"Let's do it next week..." Grace said uncertainly, feeling like a puppet on strings.

"Okay... next," Lilith called out to the man in the waiting room.

Grace looked down and walked to the exit. On the way, she accidentally bumped into the man waiting for his session.

"I'm sorry," the stranger apologized with a warm smile, his eyes kind.

She smiled back at the man, a fleeting moment of human connection, and left the room, her heart aching with a profound loneliness.

"Hello, Michael, how are things at home?" Lilith asked the man.

"It's okay, thanks. May I see Sam?" he asked respectfully.

Lilith made an inviting gesture. The man smiled and went into the room with the flowered wallpaper.

"Michael," greeted the Devil, his voice a low, dangerous purr, the room growing colder with his presence.

The archangel stepped into the room, his serene presence a stark contrast to the oppressive atmosphere. "Sam."

"Please, have a seat," the Devil invited, a predatory smile curling his lips, his eyes gleaming with malice.

Michael sat down in the cold chair, facing his brother. The room was filled with an inhuman tension, the air thick with the scent of sulfur and decay. The brothers locked eyes, the weight of millennia hanging between them. Finally, Michael spoke.

"The Father does not agree with the punishment for the girl," he said, his voice steady and unyielding, a flicker of compassion in his eyes.

"She's a sinner; the punishment is just," Samuel replied, his tone icy and unwavering, a dark satisfaction in his voice.

Michael's gaze was unwavering as he continued, "She is a sinner," he repeated, "we agree with that. However, you instilled in her a sense of guilt for the death of her parents by warning her about the accident - this is unfair."

"Father has too idealistic views," the Devil remarked, his eyes narrowing, a sneer curling his lips.

"It's hard to think otherwise when you're in an ideal world," Michael replied, a hint of warmth in his voice, his eyes softening.

Samuel passed his palm over a vase of flowers, and they quickly withered into dust, a cruel smile playing on his lips.

"This world is not perfect," the Devil demonstrated, his voice dripping with contempt, his gaze cold and unfeeling.

Michael smiled warmly, extending his hand over the vase and turning the dust back into fresh flowers, his touch gentle and life-giving.

"Your task is to teach the ideal with justice," Michael reminded, his voice gentle yet firm, a light in the darkness.

The Devil's eyes flickered with irritation as he focused on the vase. "In any case, her life belongs only to her, and only she is responsible for her actions. Her other two sins are just; we disagree only with the first one," Michael explained.

The Devil exhaled sharply, the room growing darker with his displeasure, shadows creeping along the walls. "Well, we have reached a compromise. Whose soul did the Father ask for?"

"Andrew Brown. His time has come..." Michael replied calmly, his voice a beacon of hope.

The Devil stood, the tension in the room crackling like electricity, his presence a storm of malevolence. The brothers approached each other, and despite their differences, shook hands. As their hands clasped, a ring of fire erupted around them, the flames roaring to life, a mix of hellish reds and deep blues. The fire twisted and coiled like living serpents, casting eerie shadows that danced across the room. The heat was intense, searing the air, and the light was blinding, a testament to their opposing natures.

Both were surrounded by fire and disappeared from the room with the flowered wallpaper.

—⁂—

Grace looked sadly out the window of her apartment, memories of her turbulent life flashing before her eyes. The death of her parents, quarrels with Sarah, the unrelenting bleakness... Each memory felt like a weight, pressing down on her chest. Leaning against the cold glass, she gazed at the asphalt below, desperately trying to recall her mother's smile. A tear escaped, trailing down her otherwise neutral face.

She opened the window, weighing the pros and cons of her existence. Standing on the edge, goosebumps prickled her skin. Her socks pointed downward, heels teetering for balance. She clung weakly to the window frame, feeling the pull of gravity, the allure of release from all her problems, losses, and feelings.

"Mommy!" the thought echoed in her mind, bittersweet and haunting. Grace closed her eyes, a faint smile forming as she accepted what seemed like her inevitable fate.

It felt strange to be so empty, so devoid of thought or emotion. Usually, the mind buzzed with life, with worries and dreams. Now, she felt like she was dissolving into the world around her, becoming one with the inanimate. The emptiness felt like the stillness of a corpse. Yet, abruptly, something shifted inside her. Feelings surged back, filling the void. Grace's eyes snapped open, wet with unshed tears. She no longer felt empty. A sense of wholeness, of duty, of life pulsed through her.

224

Gently, she placed a hand on her stomach. Her lips trembled into a smile, tears streaming down her face. Grace rushed to the bathroom, her hands shaking as she grabbed a pregnancy test from the medicine cabinet. She skimmed the instructions, trying to steady her breathing. Following the steps, she waited.

She paced the bathroom, glancing at the clock. Only 30 seconds had passed.

"Only 30 seconds?!" she thought, her heart pounding.

The seconds stretched into eternity. She waited, biting her thumb, nerves fraying with each passing moment. Finally, after the longest three minutes of her life, she looked at the result. Two lines…

Grace exhaled sharply, her breath catching in her throat. Tears filled her eyes. She looked up, trying to hold back the flood. A smile broke through, mixing with her tears. Relief, tension, joy, fear—all tangled together. She looked in the mirror, trying to process the whirlwind of emotions.

The world outside seemed transformed. The sun shone a bit brighter, the air felt a bit lighter. Grace touched her stomach again, feeling a new sense of purpose. The weight of her past hadn't vanished, but now there was hope, a reason to move forward.

Days turned into weeks. One evening, as she lay in bed, Grace felt a flutter. It was faint, almost imperceptible, but it was there. Her breath hitched as she pressed her hand to her stomach. There it was again, a tiny movement, the first sign of life. Her heart swelled with a mix of fear and joy. Tears welled up as she realized that a small, fragile life was growing inside her.

The feeling was overwhelming. The fear of the unknown, the worry about whether she could be a good mother, whether she could protect this tiny life. But alongside the fear was an immense joy, a profound sense of connection. She felt the flutter again, and this time, she laughed through her tears, overwhelmed by the miracle of it all.

Her thoughts raced. She wondered what kind of person her child would become, whether they would have her eyes or her mother's smile. She thought about the future, about creating a life filled with love and security for her baby. The responsibility was daunting, but she felt a fierce determination growing within her.

As the weeks passed, Grace's belly grew. She marveled at the changes in her body, at the way her baby responded to her voice, to music, to the gentle touch of her hand. Each movement was a reassurance, a reminder that she was not alone.

One night, as she lay in bed, she felt a strong kick. She gasped, her hand flying to her stomach. The kick came again, more insistent this time. She laughed, tears of joy streaming down her face. It was as if her baby was telling her, "I'm here, I'm alive, and I'm strong."

The fear was still there, lurking in the background. But a fierce love, a fierce determination to protect and nurture this new life overshadowed it. Grace knew she had a long road ahead, filled with challenges and uncertainties. But she also knew she had a reason to keep going, a reason to fight for a better future.

She looked in the mirror, seeing not just a young woman who had faced so many hardships, but a mother-to-be, strong and hopeful. She wiped away her tears, a smile on her face, and whispered to her belly, "We're going to be okay. I promise."

A bright flame lit up in the dimly lit hall. Two neatly dressed men, the Devil and the Archangel, emerged from it. Both moved with a smooth, yet confident gait. The combination of highly polished business shoes, a gray sweater, and trousers looked classically simple, but these proudly raised heads, precise steps, and fluid movements could only belong to the rulers of the world.

As they moved deeper into the hall, the sounds emanating from the doors lining the passage: bitter guttural crying, manic laughter, and suppressed screams interrupted the dead silence. The walls themselves seemed to pulse with a malevolent life, oozing a dark, viscous substance that dripped onto the floor and evaporated into foul-smelling smoke. The longer they walked, the more varied and disturbing the sounds became, yet the men continued with unflinching confidence.

Finally, stopping at a particular door, the Devil knocked. Waiting patiently for an answer, Samuel showed that respect was necessary, even in Hell. After a moment, he opened the door to the room. Michael looked around curiously. The solitary lamp on the ceiling, around which moths fluttered aimlessly, added no comfort. Papers cluttered a modest work table in the corner, and a dusty acoustic guitar stood beside it. The Archangel approached the table and examined a vase with slightly wilted flowers. The Devil moved to a wall adorned with numerous Roman numerals, reminiscent of prison tally marks.

"How long has he been here?" asked Michael.

Samuel glanced at his watch and replied, "753 years."

Michael joined his brother at the wall and began counting the crossed-out lines. "2005 attempts..." he shook his head. "Some souls find it hard to let go of the past."

A flame ignited in the room, and an elderly, well-groomed man appeared. Clad in strict clothing, with combed hair, a slight stubble, and the faint scent of cologne, Andrew entered. His eyes were haunted, reflecting years of torment.

"Hello, Andrew," the Devil greeted the sinful soul.

Andrew nodded quickly and went to the wall with the tally marks. The brothers stepped aside, allowing him to pass. A knife materialized in Andrew's hand, and he obsessively added another line.

"2006..." he whispered, counting his attempts.

"Andrew, this is my brother Michael," Sam introduced.

"Nice to meet you," Andrew said quickly, moving from the wall to the center of the room. "Wait, one more time," he requested.

With a quick gesture from Sam, the flowers bloomed again. Andrew stood with his feet shoulder-width apart, arms slightly spread. He winced in pain, and flames enveloped him, illuminating the room before leaving the brothers alone once more.

"Tell me," Michael made a gesture, and a table appeared in the room, "what is it like to retrain people?"

"I have to admit," Sam mimicked his gesture, creating two chairs, "there is some excitement in it." The Devil sat opposite his brother. "Of course, everyone eventually retrains, but I'm interested in guessing how long it will take."

"What did you think of Andrew?" the Archangel grinned.

"Honestly, I was hoping for more time," the tempter admitted.

Michael nodded understandingly and conjured two cups and a teapot on the table.

"What's it like taking people to Father?" asked Sam.

"Just like you take people to Hell," Michael replied, pouring tea into cups, "with mercy, with love, and with forgiveness." He handed a cup to the Devil.

Sam raised his glass in gratitude and sipped the hot drink. "I forget how pleasant the company of angels is," he laughed.

Michael chuckled and took a sip. "What's it like to have your own kingdom?"

"At first, I thought having a kingdom would bring me closer to Father. I was wrong. Demons caused me disappointment or disgust. Over time, I pitied them. I realized that forgiveness and acceptance, even of those you hate, even when they don't deserve it, is a great power."

"I know what you mean. We were designed to have such feelings for demons. Perhaps you are the most experienced of us," the Archangel remarked.

"Perhaps we are where we should be," Sam smiled at his brother.

A bright flame engulfed the room again, and Andrew emerged, scrawling another failure on the wall.

"Andrew, join us," the Devil invited him to the table.

He obediently sat between the brothers. "This is Michael. You may have heard of him," Sam introduced.

"Hello, sir," Andrew greeted with some apprehension, like a child greeting an adult.

"You can call me Michael," the Archangel clarified.

Andrew nodded obediently. "Well, I see a lot has changed since our last meeting," the Devil noted, pointing to Andrew's appearance and the room. "What caused these changes?"

Andrew looked at the brothers, confused. "I realized that if I want to stop using substances, I must first stop using them myself. After that, I felt disgusted by my appearance, lifestyle, and so on. So I changed."

The brothers exchanged approving glances. "After failing 2007 attempts, what have you learned?" Michael asked.

Andrew looked at the Archangel, then at Sam. "I'm afraid you were right," he said, disappointed. "I give up. I can't change myself."

"Andrew, your attempts were doomed from the start," Michael explained. "Practicing this lesson, you understand the past cannot be changed. It must be accepted."

The old man frowned, realizing the truth. "So I've wasted all this time?"

"Not at all. Do you remember yourself when you first arrived?" Sam asked.

Andrew tried to recall. "Now anger, envy, lust, and so on are alien to you. You're no longer interested in them. Anyone would let go of such thoughts after all this time in this room," the Archangel continued.

Andrew, shocked by his transformation, agreed. "What happens to me now?"

"Now, we will open your eyes," Sam said calmly.

The company found itself in a grand hall filled with people.

"Where are we?" Andrew asked, noticing the sudden change.

"At your Grammy Awards," the Archangel replied.

A woman on stage opened an envelope and joyfully announced, "Andrew Brown!"

The audience erupted in applause. A dark figure stepped onto the stage. It was twisted and grotesque, with skin like charred leather and glowing red eyes that burned with malice. Its grin was a wide, jagged maw filled with razor-sharp teeth, and black, viscous liquid dripped from its fangs.

"Who is this?" Andrew asked in horror.

"This is hatred, your greatest sin," the Devil explained. "You drew all your energy from it."

"How did I get this?" Andrew asked, pale.

"You created it yourself. Hate is the rejection of reality. You were too weak to accept your father, poverty, your girlfriend's pregnancy, and so on. You hid in hatred, burying your sincere feelings," Sam explained.

"You got rid of hate by accepting your past and forgiving everyone, including yourself," Michael added.

Andrew nodded in understanding, and the Devil waved his hand. The company returned to the original room.

"Wait," Michael said. A bright flame lit up, and the three found themselves in a dimly lit backstage area. Grime covered the walls and the air reeked with the stench of sweat and decay. A pretty girl seductively approached Andrew and attacked him with passionate kisses. The room lit up with a bright flame, and two figures emerged, the Devil and the Archangel. Sam snapped his fingers, and the girl stood frozen beside the brothers. Andrew pulled back, wiping his lips. The man looked in the mirror and instantly assumed his former, elderly, well-groomed appearance.

"Lust?" the old man asked the brothers.

"Hate. You really don't care what's between her legs. You need a sense of power and superiority. The root of all your sins is hatred," the Devil explained.

The tempter snapped his fingers once more, and the girl bared herself, revealing a grotesque and mutilated form, with no recognizable genitals or organs. After a moment, her face melted away, leaving a featureless void.

"What is it?" The old man asked in shock.

"This is a demon. You called it through a thirst for power and superiority."

"Did I take the substances out of hatred, too?" asked Andrew.

"Yes. Hate is the rejection of reality as it is. You took substances to avoid the reality of your relationship with your family and your father. You regretted in some way that you had unplanned children with a girl you didn't even imagine as their mother," the Devil finished.

Andrew lowered his eyes knowingly. Sam waved his hand, and the group returned to the original room.

"Tea?" Michael offered.

"Thank you," Andrew accepted a cup.

"Sugar?" Sam offered.

"Thank you," Andrew repeated.

He swirled his finger in the tea, but it didn't stir. Michael created a spoon and handed it to him. Andrew stirred slowly, lost in thought. After a while, he broke the silence.

"Do I still have hate in me?"

"Try to create something," Sam suggested.

Andrew waved his hand, but nothing happened. Another attempt yielded the same result. He looked questioningly at Sam.

"The room no longer obeys you," the Devil remarked, "which means you don't belong here."

The brothers stood facing each other. Andrew followed them.

"See you soon," the Devil said to the Archangel.

Michael nodded and approached Andrew with a smile, extending his hand. As their hands touched, a radiant, heavenly light enveloped them, brighter and purer than anything Andrew had ever seen. It filled him with an overwhelming sense of peace and love, banishing the darkness of Hell.

Andrew nodded, his face illuminated by the heavenly glow, and the room was bathed in the brightest warm light, leaving the Devil alone in the dim room.

A middle-aged man walked confidently through the brightly lit hall, his highly polished shoes and formal suit giving him a respectable appearance. Turning left down the corridor, he saw the inscription "dressing room." Stopping at the door to the room, the man checked his watch. The time read 11:59. The sounds of two women and one young girl came from the room.

"Aunt Grace!" a girl exclaimed in delight. "I don't even know what to say."

"Say thank you," a woman jokingly replied.

"Oh, come on, Sarah, let her be happy," another woman's voice chimed in. "I thought my Rene needed new toe shoes before the performance. Will you have time to break them in?"

"Of course!" the girl replied joyfully.

"Well, I'm off," Grace said. "I'm coming to the performance with my son, okay?"

"Mhm," came a muffled response from the room.

The man looked at his watch again; the time was now 12:00. He pressed himself against the wall and lowered his face. The door to the dressing room opened, and an elderly woman came out.

"Good afternoon," she greeted the waiting person and walked on.

The man tilted his head, not revealing his face to Grace, and watched her go. Holding the closing door, he entered the room with a bouquet of flowers in hand.

"Excuse me," he drew attention to himself. "I knew your husband, Andrew." May I talk to your daughter?" the man asked politely.

"Uh... yes, of course..." the elderly Sarah replied.

The man followed her to the next part of the dressing room, where Rene, Andrew's daughter, was trying on her new toe shoes.

"I have nothing more to say about my father, if that's what you came for," Rene snapped a little irritably.

"Hello, Rene, I did not come for your father but for you," the man politely explained, presenting the bouquet. "I brought these for you."

Rene shifted her surprised gaze to the man and then to the flowers.

"I have been watching your performances, and I am very interested in investing," the man said, smiling.

"Really?" the girl asked, still surprised.

The man grinned.

"Would you like to become the best ballet star in the world?"

Rene's eyes widened with a mix of hope and suspicion. Fame and recognition had always been her driving force, much like her father's.

The desire for adoration gnawed at her, making her feel both elated and wary.

"What do I have to do?" she asked, her voice firm.

"Just follow your true desires," the man said, extending the bouquet. "And you will have everything that you sincerely desire."

As Rene took the flowers, a flicker of doubt crossed her mind, but the intoxicating promise of success quickly overshadowed it.

The man smiled, a glint of satisfaction in his eyes. "Welcome to the path of greatness, Rene."

The girl's face lit up in awaiting happiness as she was holding the Stranger's flowers.

ABOUT THE AUTHOR

Kemal Tabyldy is a young writer, known for his novel "Stranger's Flowers". Born on May 7, 2006, in Astana, the capital of Kazakhstan, he displayed a remarkable passion for literature and the arts from an early age. He is currently a student at Columbia University in New York, where he continues to refine his craft and deepen his understanding of the literary arts and humanities.

Tabyldy's writing style has been shaped by the works of literary giants, a profound grasp of dramatic principles, and the narrative techniques often found in modern cinema and video games. This eclectic mix of influences has allowed him to forge a distinctive literary voice, blending myth, fantasy, and philosophical prose.

Known for his deep interest in the myths and legends of ancient civilizations, Tabyldy also has extensive knowledge in esotericism and theology. His works are rich with symbolism and allegory, mirroring his pursuit of exploring profound philosophical and spiritual themes. His vast erudition and insatiable curiosity about both the natural and human sciences lend his writing a complex and thought-provoking quality.

Kemal Tabyldy is an author whose work stands out for its intellectual depth and artistic finesse. His novel "Stranger's Flowers" is already garnering attention for its originality and narrative complexity, heralding a bright future for this promising young writer.

www.ingramcontent.com/pod-product-compliance
Lightning Source LLC
Chambersburg PA
CBHW050511260626

47157CB00004B/1274